THE COURTSHIP DANCE . . .

Her head spun as the marquess whisked her behind a potted palm and whirled her out onto the terrace.

"Let go of me this instant!"

"Are you afraid, Miss Bowen?" His breath caressed her neck, sending feathers of excitement along her nerves.

"How dare you! Of all the shabby conduct, this is—"

He suddenly pulled her harder against him. Amanda was aware of every muscle pressing into her. His breath tempted the soft flesh of her lips.

Before she knew what was happening to her, his mouth found hers.

THE BOOK TRADER
LA RONDE CENTRE
14806 DEL WEBB BLVD.
SUN CITY, AZ 85351

Lover's Knot

Maria Greene

JOVE BOOKS, NEW YORK

LOVER'S KNOT

A Jove Book / published by arrangement with
the author

PRINTING HISTORY
Jove edition / March 1991

All rights reserved.
Copyright © 1991 by Maria Greene.
This book may not be reproduced in whole or in part,
by mimeograph or any other means, without permission.
For information address: The Berkley Publishing Group,
200 Madison Avenue, New York, New York 10016.

ISBN: 0-515-10511-2

Jove Books are published by The Berkley Publishing Group,
200 Madison Avenue, New York, New York 10016.
The name "JOVE" and the "J" logo
are trademarks belonging to Jove Publications, Inc.

PRINTED IN THE UNITED STATES OF AMERICA

10 9 8 7 6 5 4 3 2 1

To Ray with love, as always

Lover's Knot

CHAPTER 1

"MY DEAR KEITH, I have yet to meet a female who won't snicker at my figure," Sir Digby Knottiswood complained to his nephew sitting on the opposite side of the small table. They were ensconced in two wingchairs in front of the fireplace at Sir Digby's lodgings in St. James's Street in London. A fragrant applewood fire crackled, fending off the chill of the April evening.

The nephew's strong fingers—adorned by a signet ring of black onyx—closed around the fragile stem of a brandy snifter. Lifting the glass to his eyes, Keith Marsh, the Marquess of Saville, regarded the distorted image of his portly uncle through the amber liquid, his deeply set and smoky green eyes thoughtful. "I daresay you've looked in the wrong direction, Uncle," he drawled. "There must be any number of females who would die for the chance to squander your ready." His lean face took on a brooding look as he sipped the potent liquid.

"Well, you know that I ain't able to lift the rest of my inheritance without tying the knot. Not that I have any desire to get leg-shackled—much too comfortable as it is," said Sir Digby.

A tray bearing a crystal decanter of brandy and dishes of nuts and bonbons stood at comfortable reaching distance. Sir Digby nipped a choice bonbon from the glass bowl, and with the thoroughness of a dog examining a bone, studied the chocolate oval before popping it between his fleshy lips.

"Dashed ruthless of Grandfather to tie up the blunt until you're thirty, and married to a suitable female," Lord Saville said.

Sir Digby heaved his massive shoulders. "I've lived very well on my inheritance from Mother, and I'll be thirty in a couple of months."

"But not married. I still don't understand why the old goat rated you a hothead, when I've never known a more sensible person—if a trifle timid."

Sir Digby chuckled. "He worried himself blue that I would follow in your wild footsteps, even though you're three years my junior. You cut quite a dash when you came down from Oxford and tried to pull me into mischief. You surely remember that Father highly disapproved of you. A rare stickler for propriety the old bleater was. It's still hard to believe that my starchy sister mothered a blade like you."

That provoked a rumbling laugh from the marquess. "You're right, old fellow. I must be a changeling." He took a swig of brandy and swung one long muscular leg clad in skintight pale yellow pantaloons over the other, the tassel of his exquisitely polished Hessian boot bobbing up and down.

From under his bushy eyebrows, Sir Digby regarded the striking face of his nephew, the deep brooding eyes, the aquiline nose, and the hard mouth. "This whole business is a curst nuisance. I cannot reconcile myself to the thought of giving up my peaceful life to pay attendance on some faint-hearted and giggling debutante. The mere thought is extremely distasteful."

"Who says you have to marry a debutante? You ought to seek your wife among the more mature ladies, a widow or someone who's afraid of remaining on the shelf, and desperate to wed *any* man. I know just the female for you."

Sir Digby's eyebrows pulled together in suspicion. He leaned forward threateningly. "If you're planning to commit some devilry and foist a flat-chested jaw-me-dead on me, I swear I will call you out!" To dull his fear, Sir Digby devoured three bonbons in rapid succession.

"Don't be such a pudding-heart, Dig." With a glint of amusement in his eyes, Lord Saville scoffed, "Do you take me for a complete idiot?"

Sir Digby's eyes still narrow with suspicion, he retorted, "It wouldn't be the first time you've tricked me. But, I warn you, the matter of my inheritance is serious. Without Father's legacy, I won't be able to maintain much longer the way of life to which I'm accustomed. I'm at a loss what to do to acquire it. But no matter what, you are not going to pull some prank just to get me married. You'll ruin my life."

Saville's face lit up with a slow grin. "If you reduce your food bills, you may well survive without the legacy. The only other choice is marriage."

Sir Digby gingerly patted his huge paunch, barely held in check by a Cumberland corset under the tight fit of his waistcoat. "My one passion in life," he sighed, and smacked his lips. "There is nothing like a meal prepared to perfection—slices of tender veal *au champignon* in a delicate cream sauce . . . Or the caress of thick cream flavored with arrack, generous white mounds on flaky apricot tarts." His moon-face was alight with rapture. Carefully arranged wisps of mousy brown hair, a bulbous nose, and too-large protruding ears made up the rest of his features. But there was no fault to find with the alert blue gaze he directed at his nephew. "Now then, who is the eligible female you had in mind, nevvy?" He prodded a finger at Saville's steely biceps. "And mind you, I won't tolerate a peagoose either."

"She's rather handsome in an unfashionable way, dark-haired and serious-minded. Not my taste. I'm alluding to Miss Amanda Bowen, who I'm certain will fit you to perfection. If my calculations hit the mark, this is her last chance to snare a husband. Another season without at least an engagement will destine her to taking care of her future half brothers and sisters—like a poor spinster aunt."

Sir Digby polished off the last bonbon and washed it down with a gulp of brandy. "She's not at all a bad sort, although some sparse in the chest," he said thoughtfully. "I like a soft bosom. I don't know Miss Bowen very well." He sent his nephew a keen glance, his voice taking on an edge of derision. "I take it you don't like the idea of Lurlene Bowen, your one-time fiancée, mothering Miss Amanda's half brothers and sisters."

Lord Saville stood with a jerk, his athletic body stretched to its full commanding height. A sardonic smile played on his lips. "Lurlene might have been my fiancée once, but what she does now is none of my concern." He pushed an impatient hand through his thick jet-black waves, untamed by the sweet pomades usually favored by gentlemen.

"I suppose it's the first time you've been jilted, and a world of good it does, since you're much too sure in your cockloft," Sir Digby said without rancor. "Although the whole affair has left you dashed ill-tempered of late, and it makes me bilious to witness your outbursts of rage. The devil is riding you, Keith, and you will come to a bad end if you don't cool your temper and settle down."

Lord Saville fixed his placid uncle with a jaundiced eye. "The prophet has spoken. Really, Dig, you and Miss Bowen will suit to perfection—put each other to sleep with prosy lectures."

Sir Digby clucked his tongue. "You're wrong there. It's plain you know Miss Bowen even less than I do. She shows no evidence of prosiness." He rubbed his triple chin. "What I don't understand is why she ain't married already. She must have had plenty of opportunity."

Lord Saville barked a laugh. "The chaps don't want a bluestocking for a wife. Amanda Bowen is learned and lacks the animation to snare—a sporting husband, for instance. She should have sought her mate in an Oxford don. Her lips are probably as cold as the tip of an iceberg. I've never seen her ruffled. Have you?"

"My perfect match? Is that why you think we'll suit?" Sir Digby raised a disgusted eye to his nephew's unyielding face. "Two dead bores, eh?"

Lord Saville shrugged. "You know I didn't mean that, Dig. I'm convinced she won't give you any grief in the form of a waspish tongue. And the old gargoyle Dowager Bowen will surely give Amanda a gratifying dowry. She positively dotes on the girl."

"How fortunate for me," came Sir Digby's scathing reply. "We ain't married yet, and it's unlikely she'll have me. Not every female appreciates the advantage of a substantial man to protect her—although I'm not as fast-moving as I once was." From habit, he mopped his brow with a folded handkerchief. "But I ain't a spavined horse either."

Lord Saville seemed lost in thought.

Sir Digby glared at his silent nephew. "And there's nothing wrong with book-learning. I like a sensible female. Perhaps you should fix your interest with some lady. It's high time you set up your nursery. We could celebrate a double wedding. Too bad Olivia Lexington appears to favor Wrexham. Now that's a charming female."

Lord Saville made a grunt of disgust. "I have no intention of marrying."

"Don't be ridiculous, Keith! You were betrothed to Lurlene not too long ago. You'll find someone else soon."

Sir Digby missed the misery in his nephew's eyes as the younger man averted his face. He might have regretted his well-intentioned words had he but seen into the depths of Lord Saville's mind and the plans that were brewing there.

Sir Digby's voice grew jocular as he sensed his nephew's sudden mood change. "You could have anyone, Keith. All the debutantes are dying for a glance from you."

When the marquess responded, the broodiness had gone, and he chuckled. "Painting me irresistible, are you, Dig? How kind. I've managed to evade matrimony this far, so I'll manage somehow to stay unwed in the future," he said. "But I will gladly assist *you* into a parson's mousetrap."

Sir Digby squeezed a finger between his high stiff shirtpoints and his thick neck in an effort to relieve the pressure of the tight neckcloth. "Hmm, how would I go about catching Miss Bowen's attention?"

"Child's play. You'll start by sending her flowers every day to show that your interest is more than friendly. I wager she'll be bowled over with excitement. In a week's time we'll be at some function she's bound to attend, and *voilà*, there you fix your interest. Mark my words, the little dark mouse will be thrilled to have a suitor at last."

Sir Digby looked skeptical. "One that weighs nineteen stone?"

"Don't doubt it! You're a most agreeable fellow despite your considerable bulk, and she'll notice your kindness and pleasant manners. Remember—she's desperate."

"Oh, blister me! Just the thought of the ordeal ahead makes me famished." Sir Digby heaved himself with difficulty out of his chair and tottered to the bellrope by the fireplace. "I'm going to order a small meal to carry me through to dinner. Will you join me, nevvy? My chef cooks up some very tolerable dishes, if only a snack."

"Sounds tempting, old fellow, but I have a previous engagement at White's. But remember to order an armful of roses delivered to Miss Bowen's door first thing in the morning."

Sir Digby nodded, conjuring up the images of a small juicy pigeon pie and a gooseberry tart with vanilla custard. And perhaps a bottle of claret to wash it all down. . . .

Lord Saville tweaked the faultless folds of his neckcloth tied in the *Trône d'Amour* style, and critically viewed the fit of his coat in the mirror above the fireplace. Leaning heavily on his cane, he limped cautiously through the antique furniture that Sir Digby collected, to the door.

A stern-faced valet materialized at Saville's side and handed him a beaver hat and yellow kid gloves.

"Thank you, Keith. I knew I could count on you to find an answer to my problem," Sir Digby sent after the retreating figure.

Miss Amanda Bowen moved in blissful ignorance of Sir Digby's plans for her future as she began dressing for an evening at the Royal Italian Opera House in Haymarket. She was to accompany her father, Lord Justin Bowen, and his new wife, Lurlene.

In her grandmother's elegant South Street townhouse, behind a screen in her bedchamber, Amanda leaned over a washbasin and washed her slight body.

She heard her maid, Meg, an indomitable Irishwoman

who had been with her charge since Amanda drew her first breath, laying out an evening gown on the bed.

"Is that the white muslin slip with the silver net tunic? It is very stylish, don't you think?" Amanda mused aloud and slathered soap on her arms.

"Fat lot o' good it does!" Meg scoffed. "No gen'leman has noticed ye."

"One day, Meg, someone will. I'm waiting for the right man, and will not settle for anything less than true love," Amanda said lightly.

"That sweet tone doesn't fool me," the maid said. "True love, indeed. Bah!"

Amanda hummed a tune as she rinsed her slender arms and graceful neck. "I'm not planning on impressing anyone tonight, but I can still like my new gown, can't I?"

She ignored Meg's following snort, and her thoughts returned to Lurlene and the likelihood of her stepmother spoiling a perfectly good evening with her endless chatter. However, a wave of anticipation rolled through Amanda at the thought of hearing La Catalani perform in *Semiramide*. As long as she could turn a deaf ear to Lurlene, the evening promised to be pleasurable.

For her poor father's sake she struggled to conquer her dislike of her new stepmama. But it proved to be a constant battle, and she was steadily losing ground. Lurlene, eighteen years old and four years Amanda's junior, habitually gloated over the fact that Amanda wasn't yet married. It hurt Amanda more every day to be the target of Lurlene's stinging barbs.

She sighed and slipped her shift over her head. After locating her stockings under a towel on a low stool, she stepped out from behind the screen. The room was decorated in pale green and gold with Louis XV furniture polished to the color of rich honey. Thick carpets with a lively pattern of Chinese dragons spewing fire—the only concession Grandmama had made to the madness for Oriental decor—cuddled her bare feet. A bouquet of daffodils sweetened the air, reminding her of the summer to come, even though a cold wind rattled the windows. The season of the *haut monde* was barely underway.

She pushed a hand through her mahogany curls, shaking off a few stray drops of water. Staring with longing at a history book lying beside her hairbrush, she knew her reading would have to wait. Grandmama said she had an unhealthy interest in the past, but Amanda couldn't think of anything more fascinating than the events that had brought England to where it was today.

The talk she had had with Grandmama that afternoon still haunted Amanda. Perhaps her grandmother was right about the urgency of finding a husband this season. Amanda heaved a sigh. She had no desire to make a hasty marriage, but she also disliked the idea of sponging off the dear old griffin for the rest of her life. And to stay with Father and Lurlene at Bowen House in Berkley Square was unthinkable. There was no perfect solution. Not only that, but having a serious disposition, Amanda knew she had gained the reputation of being somewhat of a scholar. Sighing, she sought her slippers under the chair by the dressing table. She liked many things, but the gentlemen overlooked her riding skills, her love for music, her interest in fashion, and only saw the word BLUESTOCKING painted across her forehead.

A rap on the door interrupted her thoughts. As she slipped on a lace-edged silk petticoat, she heard Meg turn the doorknob.

"Amanda's still here then," the Dowager Lady Bowen said. In louder, slightly injured tones, "I want a word with you, miss, before you leave me to pay attendance on *that woman.*"

Amanda smiled, and tore off a loose thread in the seam of the silk. Gesturing with white satin slippers in one hand and silk stockings in the other, she invited her grandparent to sit down on the chair by the fire. "Don't worry, Grandmama, I won't let Lurlene treat me like a slave." She sank down on the chair in front of her dressing table to let Meg brush her hair, a chore the maid embarked upon with vigor.

The Dowager tottered across the carpet and settled on the chair, her razor-sharp gaze following Meg's every move. She had a perfectly clear view of Amanda's delicate features in the glass—the wide slanted eyes above high cheekbones, the small, slightly retroussé nose, the boldly curved lips, the crown of short curls, and the stubborn chin. Amanda's face was lovely, if only she didn't look so *bookish*, the Dowager thought with a sigh. It daunted the gentlemen. They never looked farther than simpering faces and trim figures. Her granddaughter had the kindest of dispositions, but she much too seldom dared to open up and show her inner animation. She needed someone to draw her out of her shell. And her coloring wasn't fashionable. No, pink and white it had to be today—all fluttering eyelashes and affected smiles. Faugh!

With an impatient gesture the Dowager said, "Meg, pull some of those curls over the chit's forehead to conceal that intelligent look. Men abhor intelligence in a female." Then she crowed mercilessly. "At least Mandy isn't a feather-brain, like *that woman*. I swear I have never been more shocked than when Justin announced he was going to marry *her*!"

Amanda raised amused eyes of dusky darkness from the open jewel case to study her grandparent's angry face. "Dearest Grandmama, it's no use stewing over things of the past. Lurlene surely loves Father and vice versa."

The Dowager jabbed her cane into the head of a dragon on the carpet underfoot. "Every day we have to live with the humiliating knowledge that your father made an idiot of himself. Even though he is my son, I could throttle him with my bare hands. And your poor mother dead only these two years."

"You couldn't kill a fly, and well you know it," Amanda said firmly, attempting to hide the stab of sorrow piercing her as she remembered her gentle mother. She bent her gaze to the task of selecting suitable jewelry.

"Saucy minx," the Dowager rejoined. "If anything positive can be said about the matter, Justin wasn't the first to make a cake of himself at Lurlene's door. I guess the run was close between him and that whipstraw Saville. Not that I understand why she chose my Justin over Lord Saville, who is not only five and twenty years Justin's junior, but also very plump in the pocket. And"—she stabbed the air with one finger—"Lurlene would have been permitted to wear the coronet of a Marchioness. That is nothing to turn up one's nose at."

Amanda fought with the tiny screw of one earring. "Well, rumor has it that Lord Saville is still madly in love with her."

The Dowager pursed her lips into the shape of a prune. "Then he's more of a chawbacon than I imagined. Some other miss should have a chance at his pockets this season, but if he's still carrying the torch for *that woman*, then matchmaking mamas should look elsewhere. There is less flamboyant prey abroad ready for plucking."

Amanda sighed wearily. "You make matchmaking sound so heartless—like a fox hunt. You must have some compassion under all that grumpiness."

Ignoring all allusion to compassion, the Dowager replied, "A hunt is the precise word. One has to approach the subject with cunning, finesse and subtlety." Breathing hard, a rasping resentful sound, she tapped her kid half-boot on the floor and eyed a stack of history books with disdain.

"I think you're being unfair to the poor gentlemen, Grandmama."

"That's only because you see men as people. They are Conquests, my dear—Conquests! Without wile you'll fail to snare one of their species, and in that department you could learn a great deal from your new stepmama."

"If I ever marry, it'll be for love," Amanda claimed, raising her chin.

"Fustian! In our circle you don't marry for love. The blame lies, as usual, in your father's dish for not pairing you up with an eligible gentleman instead of acting like a veritable greenhorn by running after that insipid Lurlene."

Amanda chuckled. "She's excessively beautiful. Her golden hair and pink complexion are all the rage this season, and her blue eyes are the sapphires glorified in every poet's verse," she said without an apparent trace of envy.

"Lurlene is like a cold soufflé—or a blancmange," the Dowager said gruffly.

Amanda thoughtfully pulled one of her short ebony curls behind her ear, and cocked a rounded eyebrow, the black bow startling against her pale translucent skin. "What did you want to see me about?" she asked. "I'm sure you didn't bestir yourself only to comment on my coiffure and rant about Lurlene."

"No—as a matter of fact, I have some news that will please you greatly. My witch of a sister, Elfina, is finally allowing my grandniece a trip to London to try her luck at the Marriage Mart."

"Pamela? Coming here?" Amanda leaped from her chair in a flurry of delight. Lady Pamela Waring was Amanda's cousin and childhood friend. "Splendid! Only imagine how Pam must have begged Lady Waring to allow her a season here in London, a place the old lady considers to be a giant fleshpot." Amanda impulsively embraced her grandmother, who instantly pushed her away.

"Enough of this twaddle." The Dowager sniffed and looked at Amanda from the corner of her eye. "I'm going to bring her out. You'll be very busy squiring her around to all the sights and shops. We have to make the most of it now that Elfina has let Pamela out of her clutches. In fact, I might just insist Pamela stay for a whole year—that is, if she doesn't find a husband before you do."

"Oh, Grandmama, why this tedious talk about finding husbands? You never speak of anything else." In the next breath Amanda once more flung out her arms with pleasure at the thought of Pamela's imminent arrival. "We're going to entertain her royally."

The Dowager was already making her way toward the door, her stiff knees creaking with every step. "Remember what I said, Amanda. The both of you'll have a very busy season, *husband hunting*."

"Grandmama, you're impossible."

Standing in the doorway, the Dowager wagged a censoring finger. "You'd better be the first to get married, and he'd better be a man of consequence."

"Who do you consider up to par, Grandmama?" Amanda asked shrewdly, but the only response she got was a malicious cackle from the hallway.

Amanda brooded in silence; the future looked grim indeed.

CHAPTER 2

AMANDA REGARDED her father, the baron, fondly as he stepped into the hallway of the Dowager's house in South Street. He certainly looked much younger than his forty-eight years, she mused. He was wearing full evening attire of satin knee-breeches, silk stockings, pumps, an immaculate black tailcoat with double-notched lapels which austerely framed his complicated neckcloth-folds.

His steps were buoyant, his face still firm, and his mobile mouth was prone to laughter. His brown curls without a hint of gray lay coaxed and pomaded forward into the fashionable Brutus style and his blue eyes smiled down on Amanda.

"Are you ready, my dear?" He offered a supporting arm, and Amanda placed her hand lightly on his sleeve while pulling her embroidered cashmere shawl closer around her shoulders with the other. "Yes, Papa."

"You look adorable. That new short haircut becomes you very well, Mandy," commented Lord Bowen, displaying his appreciation for female elegance as he led her down the front steps. Amanda was wearing her new high-waisted

white muslin gown with tiny puffed sleeves. The misty
tunic of loosely woven silver thread gleamed in the shifting
light. A silver ribbon wound in and out of her curls, and
pearl drops adorned her ears. Mustering up a smile, she
braced herself for the inevitable encounter with her stepmother in the carriage.

"There you are, Amanda," came a silky female voice
from the interior of the carriage. As Amanda settled her
dress carefully around her on the seat, Lurlene added with
obvious distaste, "Haven't I seen that gown before? *I*
wouldn't dare to be caught in the *faux pas* to be seen in the
same dress more than once." She shuddered delicately. "I
would never want to be the victim of such a terrible
tragedy."

Amanda forced down her flare of anger and greeted her
stepmama pleasantly. "Good evening, Lurlene. You must
recall that you were at Madame Colette's when this was
fitted last week."

Lurlene shrugged and looked out the window with
supreme indifference. The outing was already off to a bad
start. The coach rumbled down South Street toward Park
Lane.

"I hope you're well," Amanda said with an inaudible
sigh.

"As well as one can be in view of the expected crush at
the Opera. In my condition—" Lurlene fell to whipping a
fan back and forth in front of her face.

Amanda drew her breath sharply at the information subtly
thrown at her. Her eyes searched her father's face automatically, and he squirmed with certain embarrassment. "Condition?" she breathed.

"Yes-er, you'd have to find out sooner or later, Mandy."
He fumbled for her hand and squeezed it tightly. "Lurlene
is in the family way," he blurted out. His eyes were like

those of a begging dog, and Amanda swallowed the immediate outraged retort on her tongue.

"Well, I'm stunned!" It took tremendous effort to pat Lurlene's gloved hand. "I hope you're not over-taxing yourself."

Lord Bowen laughed. "No, she's strong as a horse."

Lurlene sent him a disapproving glance. "How very crude an expression, Justin. It would be enough to say that I'm in the best of health."

She did radiate a secret purr, Amanda thought, wishing she didn't feel shut out from their happiness. It had been a big step to place the care of her father into Lurlene's hands, and now he was moving even farther away by creating a new family.

"Now, don't get into a twitter, Amanda. I know this is not the best of times to reveal our glorious news, but you'll soon get used to the idea of a small half brother," Lurlene gushed.

Amanda seized the edge of her seat. "What if it's a girl?" she asked with a tremble in her voice.

Lurlene raised her nose in frigid hauteur. "I *know* 'tis a boy."

Amanda suppressed a sudden laugh. This is ridiculous, she thought, and the sore knot in her chest dissolved. *Poor Papa. Why doesn't he see Lurlene's vanity?* "I expect you know what you're talking about."

"We will retire to Bowen Court after the season to await the infant's arrival. I hope you'll consider going with us," Lord Bowen said, worry tinting his voice.

Although she didn't want to hurt her father's feelings, Amanda was relieved to have a perfectly good excuse to decline the invitation. "Grandmama will need me to entertain Pamela Waring. She's coming up to London for the season."

Lord Bowen laughed. "Elfina must be losing her iron grip if she lets her only lamb come to this den of iniquity."

"Grandmama is bent on finding Pam a husband." Amanda refrained from informing them that she too was included in the old dear's matrimonial campaign.

Lurlene's face took on a calculating air. "It won't be difficult to find a husband for that pretty widgeon. She has a large inheritance."

Amanda knew Pamela would fume if she ever found out that Lurlene had called her a widgeon. "Grandmama was busy all day mulling over various candidates, but I'm certain Pamela will have *her* say in the matter. After all, she managed to persuade Great-aunt Elfina to let go of her leading strings at last—some great victory."

Lurlene eyed her frostily through the gloom of the carriage. "I'm sure Pamela has no idea who is suitable, so we must do our best to prevent her from falling into the clutches of some encroaching mushroom or other gentleman beyond the pale." She spread out her hands to study the multitude of glittering rings on her begloved fingers. "She couldn't have better connections, naturally."

Amanda knew her stepmother was referring to herself, and she swallowed a heated reply. Irritation was always part of any outing with Lurlene.

Fortunately the carriage soon halted in front of the Opera House. Justin led his ladies under the wide arched portico to the doors, where they soon melded into the crush of patrons eagerly pushing forward to find their seats.

Upon entering the roomy box her father had subscribed for the season, Amanda relaxed. The box was on the second tier, and she lifted her small golden binoculars to view the gorgeously appareled and bejeweled ladies in the other boxes. She recognized the Duchesses Richmond and Argyll, and the Ladies Melbourne and Jersey, whose even more dazzling neighbors surely were "Fashionable Impures." Not that Amanda was supposed to know about the darker side of society, but after four years in London, she could easily distinguish between the real and the so-called ladies. The gall of highborn gentlemen to flaunt their light o' loves right under the noses of their wives!

"I'm sure I've seen Lady Jersey in that tasteless rag before, and she always wears those horrid diamond earrings," Lurlene said in an undertone, staring through her own opera glasses. "How very common."

Lurlene was evidently comparing her own outfit to those of their high-ranking neighbors. She looked stunning in an empire silk gown of palest pink with a tunic of sheer white lace, her golden curls arranged *à la Grecque*, and her face flushed.

Amanda let her gaze travel down to the pit where several fops and dandies were making a great nuisance of themselves, showing off their clothes, and talking loudly in affected voices while snapping the lids of their snuffboxes.

At the edge of her vision she became aware of a gentleman limping into the pit. He stopped just inside the door and lifted a quizzing glass to one eye, scanning the occupants of the boxes. He was more than just handsome—positively dangerous—despite his limp. His suave elegance could not conceal the virile magnetism that seemed to exude from his every pore.

His perusal ceased at their box. His brief piercing glance forced a sudden hot prickly sensation through Amanda's body, and she winced, instinctively pulling back in her chair.

In a daze she heard Lurlene's soft laughter. "He's here, just like he said he would be."

"Who?" Amanda heard herself ask, but she knew very well to whom her stepmother was referring.

"Keith, of course; Lord Saville." Lurlene made no secret about it. "He's still dangling after me, y' know."

"Then he has more hair than wit, since you're happily married and out of his reach." Amanda looked again at the magnificent man on the floor below them. Something in her chest tightened as she reminded herself that a man like Lord Saville would never look at her twice. He bowed his dark head a fraction, and through her spyglass, Amanda saw the sardonic tilt of his lips. She studied his evening dress, the black well-cut coat striking against the hard planes of his face. The intricate neckcloth folds rivaled those of Beau Brummell himself, the absolute arbiter of fashion.

When no answer but a sigh of longing was forthcoming from Lurlene, Amanda slanted a glance toward her young stepmama. "You don't encourage him, do you?" she asked, grateful that her father had absented himself to fetch refreshments from the lounge.

"Well, I almost married him, y'know." Lurlene tittered with excitement, and made a beckoning sign to Lord Saville, for the whole world to see.

"You can't invite him up here! Father will have a fit if he finds out that you still have an eye for the marquess." Amanda's face burned with humiliation, and she was well aware that a multitude of opera glasses were aimed in their direction, as an entrance by, or a glance from the Marquess of Saville never went unnoticed. But Saville did not respond; he limped down the aisle to speak with the rotund Sir Digby Knottiswood who stood in conversation with an acquaintance.

At least the annoying man wasn't trotting to their box. Fuming, Amanda ignored the many curious glances, and trained her glasses on the stage where *Semiramide* was about to start. But she saw nothing. She was painfully aware of Lord Saville's presence, and her own inexplicable emotion—the jolting of her senses as if she had sustained a shock. How dare he openly acknowledge his attachment to Lurlene by singling her out with his eyes!

The sound of La Catalani's famous voice went into one of Amanda's ears and out the other, and her failure to concentrate irked her. She had so looked forward to the performance of the opera singer.

In the intermission, their box filled with Lurlene's admirers. To be polite, the gentlemen directed several remarks to Amanda without really noticing her, and she murmured suitable responses. They basked in the sun of Lurlene's dazzling smile. Amanda didn't blame the gentlemen for being entranced with her stepmother, whom at first glance seemed to be sweetness incarnate. Amanda almost wished that her father could witness the false smiles Lurlene bestowed on these fops, but he had gone to pay his respects to the family of an old friend in another box.

A hush fell over the gentlemen and Amanda's gaze darted to the door of their box. Aggravation rolled through her as her eyes locked with the scorching green gaze of Lord Saville. The insolence of the man, to make an appearance in their box!

To her surprise, he didn't immediately saunter forth to pay his respects to "Queen" Lurlene. With his eyeglass he favored Amanda with a thorough scrutiny, one that made her want to sink through the floor. Lurlene impatiently called his name when she became aware of the undue notice he paid her stepdaughter.

"Keith! Where are your manners? You're embarrassing poor Amanda with your naughty stare," she said with a come-hither voice.

Amanda wrenched her gaze from his demonic eyes. Her knuckles whitened with the strain of clutching the fringe of her shawl, and she forced herself to relax. But she couldn't

stop herself from glowering as Lord Saville's sensual lips
brushed Lurlene's hand.

"Keith, you sly dog! Are you trying to make me jealous
by giving so much attention to Amanda?" Lurlene droned
on, tapping him on the arm with her fan. Amanda sensed
that he was once again looking at her. A slow blush crept
unbidden over her body. His presence provoked her out of
her usual quiet calm, but feigning indifference, she raised
her opera glasses.

"Enjoying the caterwauling of La Catalani, Miss Bowen?"

Amanda's emotions boiled. "She's supreme," she said in
a very soft voice, fixing him with a withering stare. "But if
you cannot enjoy her voice, perhaps you're at the wrong
place altogether."

Her words drew guffaws from the assembled gentlemen,
and a sarcastic smile played over the marquess's lips as his
thumb caressed the smooth gold surface of his snuffbox.
"Egad, your contempt has mortally wounded me."

"Come now, Keith. Does teasing Amanda give you such
pleasure?" Lurlene demanded peevishly, batting her eyelashes.

"I don't recall goading her, only asking a civil question,"
he said in smooth tones. But if he hoped to break Amanda's
composure, he failed. She turned flashing eyes on him, her
shoulders tense.

"Calling La Catalani's extraordinary voice caterwauling
is hardly civil," she reminded him. "I suppose you're
ignorant when it comes to the finer points of music." Her
words reaped another round of laughter from the spectators.
Deeply shaken, Amanda wondered how she dared to speak
so discourteously. He brought out the worst in her; but then
he was so insufferably arrogant.

"Amanda!" Lurlene's voice barely penetrated the red

haze fogging Amanda's brain, and she refused to back down from the green deadly glitter of his eyes. Swallowing convulsively, she felt embarrassment seep through her as their eyes fought, but she stiffened her spine. Flushed and tight of lip, he murmured, "I say!"

"Botheration, Saville," someone said, breaking the spell, and their battle of wills ended as they lowered their eyes simultaneously. "You're in an odd temper this evening."

Lord Saville shrugged. "What can I say when a beautiful lady makes mincemeat of me? I was merely making an innocent effort to entertain Miss Bowen," he said in deceptively dulcet tones.

He had neatly turned the tables on her, but Amanda's ire when raised, was formidable.

"If you consider your bored comment to be entertainment, you must have very little to say for yourself." Aiming to intimidate him, she raised her opera glasses to stare at him, while her body trembled with the dare. To her surprise he chuckled.

"Did you hear that, my friends? Miss Bowen's razor-edged comments easily put Mr. Brummell's vitriolic tongue in the shade. Miss Bowen, you're a true descendant of the old Dowager Bowen, all the way to your dainty slippers." He raked his gaze from her curly head to the hem of her gown, and rubbed his jutting chin thoughtfully. "You completely overturn my old opinion of you."

"Opinion? How could you have formed one, since we've never spoken above five words to each other?" To Amanda's chagrin, she felt her cheeks redden with mortification.

"I have eyes in my head—"

"I wonder," Amanda retorted.

"You—er, seemed a most amenable person."

"Conceited people usually come to hasty conclusions," she rejoined.

"Amanda! What has gotten into you? Don't listen to her, Keith. She's usually so well-behaved. Where is Justin? I think I shall have a fit of the vapors," Lurlene wailed. She placed a hand to her forehead in a tragic gesture that could have rivaled one of La Catalani's.

Amanda plied her fan rapidly in front of Lurlene's face while the spectacle was followed with gluttonous interest by people in the neighboring boxes. She had another blistering comment on her tongue when, at last, her father reappeared.

Lady Bowen's admirers hastened to surge out the door, all except Lord Saville, who propped his back against the wall, still toying with his snuffbox. He watched Lord Bowen with an indifferent eye. Amanda's father gave him a questioning glare, and the air snapped with tension.

"What is going on here?" Bowen asked.

"It's Amanda," Lurlene whimpered, and Amanda wanted to push her stepmother over the padded railing of the box.

She refused to meet her father's glance. She pinched her lips together and gathered her reticule and gilded program.

"Your daughter has a ready tongue in her head, Bowen," drawled Lord Saville.

Lord Bowen studied Amanda with some surprise before turning his attention once more to Lurlene. A frown of worry creased his brows. "I think it's time to go home," he ordered the wilting wife, and Amanda blessed the signal that the second act was about to start.

Lord Saville stepped forward to place the soft shawl across Amanda's shoulders. His touch scalded her through the thin material of her gown, making her blood race through her veins. Her mind whirled in confusion, and she was disgusted with her passionate reaction to his odious touch.

Then he bowed stiffly, a veiled look in his eyes, before

holding the door for her. She cringed away to avoid him as she stepped into the corridor.

"Good night, Miss Bowen," he murmured behind her.

She hurried away, all the time feeling his gaze on her back.

After the brightly lit theatre, she was grateful for the darkness of the carriage. Certain that everybody had noticed her humiliation, Amanda wanted nothing more than to hide in the sanctuary of her home.

Lurlene sobbed weakly against Lord Bowen's shoulder. "You s-should have heard h-her—Keith said that her comments were more c-cutting than those of Mr. Brummell, and you know that no one has a more a-abrasive disposition than h-he. I've never been more embarrassed in my life. Amanda behaved like a veritable *harpy*. I don't know what got into her. She took a violent dislike to Keith and insulted him in the most blistering of manners."

Unable to stifle a few words of truth, Amanda said, "I recall that Lord Saville was less than civil."

"But you started it! You know that La Catalani does nothing but torture eardrums, and he was only making a polite remark to that effect."

"I beg to differ on that score, Lurlene, and you—" Amanda bit her tongue. Without causing her father unnecessary grief, how could she reveal that her stepmother had invited Lord Saville to their box? Sooner or later he would fall from his blissful pink cloud and see his young bride for what she really was—a spoilt brat!

"What got into you, Amanda? I have nothing good to say about Lord Saville, but he's very influential. If you raise his ire, he'll see to it that you never dance at the balls again. Would you like to be frozen from polite society?" Her father's voice lectured her, and she silently cursed his blind devotion to the odious Lurlene. He would never hear the truth, no matter how many times she explained what had really happened.

"My life certainly doesn't rise and fall with that—that—" she remembered the Dowager's expression for the likes of Lord Saville—"*whipstraw!*" But her words only created more hysteria on Lurlene's part.

"See, Justin, didn't I tell you? She's becoming as bad as the Dowager. I don't understand why you let her live with that old fossil."

Amanda's eyes shot icy sparks and she dared her father to defend his own mother, but he only shrugged and patted Lurlene benignly on her cheek. "I agree Mother is a handful, but surely Amanda isn't anywhere near as bad as she."

Amanda expelled a shuddering breath as the carriage came to a halt in front the Dowager Lady Bowen's tall, narrow house. "Don't bother to descend, I can get down alone. Anyway, Billings is undoubtedly waiting up for me."

One of the footmen opened the door to the carriage and handed her down, and the ancient butler was waiting at the top of the stairs.

"Good night, Papa." Firmly closing the door behind her, Amanda hurried into the house.

"I gather the evening was cut somewhat short," Billings commented. "But I take the liberty to surmise you'll be very pleased to hear that Lady Pamela has arrived, Miss Amanda."

CHAPTER 3

Lady Pamela was sound asleep when Amanda peeped into the Blue guestroom. Not having the heart to awaken her, Amanda quietly closed the door and sought the tranquillity of her own bedroom.

Yet once in her bed, she spent most of the night tossing and turning as her dreams were haunted by the face and mocking smile of a certain arrogant lord.

When she descended the stairs the next morning, her eyes burned and her head ached. But something out of the ordinary soon snatched her attention away from her torment.

A huge bouquet of red roses adorned the Chippendale table in the hallway. Who had sent them? Inhaling the intoxicating scent of the flowers, her heart careening, Amanda withdrew the gilt-edged card from among the stems. "To Miss Bowen, the exquisite flower of my heart. Sir Digby Knottiswood."

She drew a shocked breath, dropping the card on the table. *Sir Digby?* He had never shown any particular interest in her, and now this. Dismayed, she stared at the still-dewy flowers, so velvety and rich in color. She remembered that he had glanced repeatedly at their box last night, but so had a host of others. She stared unseeing at her reflection in the gilt girandole mirror above the flowers. What was the meaning of this?

She heard the Dowager's cane attack the parquet floor behind her, and she turned, bewilderment blurring her gaze. "Is this part of your husband-hunting scheme, Grandmama?" she asked, waving the card under the Dowager's jutting nose.

Without answering Amanda's question, the Dowager inspected the roses with maddening thoroughness. "Whoever sent these, is no skinflint. I suppose Pamela has a secret admirer who knows she's here."

"Albeit hard to believe, they are for me," Amanda said, nettled, and thrust the card into the Dowager's bony hand.

Settling onto a gilded chair, the old lady lifted the eyeglass that hung on a velvet ribbon around her neck and studied the card with avid interest. "Sir Digby Knottiswood. . . . Never did fancy him to be in the petticoat line. He has been wed to his dinner table these ten years or more." The black watered silk of her dress crackled as she fidgeted on the chair. "How odd."

"He has never shown me the slightest interest, other than casual friendship." Amanda frowned in concentration, trying to resolve this unexpected riddle. "And I don't recall him ever courting any particular female."

"Ha! He's been very comfortable with his various Cyprians these many years, I'll warrant. How they tolerate that huge paunch of his, I don't know." The old dowager cackled and flapped her enormous black and gold fan back and forth. Her sharp eyes twinkled mischievously.

"Grandmama! You're forgetting yourself." Amanda's lips quivered, and her dark eyes sparkled.

"It's no secret, and you're not a squeamish sort of female to faint at a few stark truths about this wicked world." The Dowager eyed her granddaughter with new respect. "Perhaps 'tisn't too late to hope for a husband for you, after all. But I cannot abide Sir Digby's figure."

Exasperated, Amanda flung herself onto another chair at the opposite side of the hallway, next to a small table holding a hideous gilt statuette and another flower arrangement of daffodils and pussy willows. The walls were adorned by portraits of Bowen forefathers and a moth-eaten tapestry that, according to the Dowager, had hung at Hampton Court during Queen Elizabeth's reign.

Amanda viewed the roses with suspicion. "You're talking as if Sir Digby were a horse to be set through his paces."

"Very well put, my dear. He's not a bad suitor to have dangling at your apron-strings. You could do much worse than Sir Digby Knottiswood. Now you only have to pretend indifference to incense his ardor."

"What gall! How can you be so callous? I don't intend to marry Sir Digby—although I find his attention rather amusing. Grandmama, how many times do I have to tell you that I'm perfectly capable of handling my own affairs?" Amanda rose with a swish of pale yellow muslin skirts. "Let's have breakfast before I say something I will regret— like I did last night." Too late did she realize her mistake. Already the Dowager's curiosity was palpable in the room.

"What did you say? What happened?" Old but strong fingers gripped Amanda's arm, and she had to bear the slight weight of her grandmother as they slowly walked into the breakfast parlor at the back of the house.

"Tell me before the servants arrive," the Dowager demanded. "They have ears like empty pails."

Amanda sighed. There was no stopping now. "I insulted Lord Saville." Reliving their heated exchange, she exclaimed, "I've never been more furious in my life! He came, as cool as you please, to our box, to court Lurlene when Papa was elsewhere. And she, in front of every cat with two eyes, encouraged him."

The Dowager frowned. "Really? Well, I hope you gave him his comeuppance, and with interest."

"I did, and I'm sure the episode must be on everyone's tongues this morning. Gossip travels fast."

"Hmm, if your conduct at the Opera is the topic discussed at every breakfast table in Mayfair this morning, it might make Sir Digby hesitate to send you any more roses." The Dowager gave a bark of laughter. "But I wish I had been there to see it. Saville needs to be taken down a notch or two—has always been too toplofty as it is. Mandy, my dear Mandy, I'm glad you dared to voice your thoughts for once." In glee, she slapped Amanda's forearm with her fan.

"Unfortunately, he gave as good as he got," Amanda admitted grudgingly.

The old Dowager chuckled, setting the plumes dancing in her silver curls. "That must have been priceless entertainment, much better than that mewing Italian, whom I cannot abide."

Amanda helped her grandmother to get settled at the table. "Then you share Lord Saville's opinion about the Italian singer." She grimaced with chagrin. "That started off the whole episode—his dislike for La Catalani." Amanda sat down at her place, at the opposite end of the table.

They were interrupted by the entrance of Billings, who filled the Dowager's cup with tea and Amanda's with coffee. Amanda hungrily bit into her toast. From the sideboard, the appetizing smell of fried eggs, ham and kippers enticed her nostrils, and Amanda asked Billings to serve her a plate of eggs.

Between bites, the Dowager muttered thoughtfully, "I daresay Saville has a few agreeable points. Even you, Amanda, cannot be entirely immune to his devilishly handsome face and mysterious limp. They say he received a bullet in his leg, but no one knows how or why. A duel, I wager, since Saville is so close-mouthed about it. The pain would be enough to make him sour. However, I wager he's not as ill-tempered and cheeseparing as was the old Lord Saville."

"I didn't know you knew him." Amanda filled her fork with eggs, eager to find out more about Lord Saville.

"Oh, yes, I've always known the Savilles." Stirring her tea, the Dowager rambled on. "His mother was a beautiful woman, with such style. She married old sour Saville, a move I suspect she regretted later. He is a terrible old stick, living like a recluse since his wife's death. The mother died in a coaching accident a few years back." She laughed. "Now, the old Duchess Ashborough, Keith's grandmother, was a busybody of the worst kind. In our heyday she had a reputation of being *fast*—and I believe she was, although she somehow managed to lure the Duke of Ashborough into matrimony. I think Keith takes after that old harpy." She sighed and stirred her cup absently. "We were sprightly in those days, never had a boring moment. Young Keith has few close relatives left, and Sir Digby is one. Keith's starchy sister is married to a Frog and must be fearing for her life in that beehive across the Channel." The Dowager's voice droned on, moving into other memories that had nothing to do with the Savilles. Amanda listened with only half an ear. She glanced at the clock on the sideboard, waiting impatiently for Pamela to join them. Half an hour passed, along with two generations of gossip, before she heard Pamela's timid step in the hallway.

Pushing back her chair, Amanda rose to embrace the

younger woman. "What an age!" she exclaimed. "Let me look at you." Holding Pamela at arm's length, she studied her friend. "You look your usual happy self, and so pretty." And she meant every word.

Pamela gave her a slight push, laughter dancing in her hazel eyes. "Don't bamboozle me! You must see that my hair has no style and my gown is old as Methuselah."

That was true. Even though Pamela's outmoded gown was faded, the lovely girl radiated such vigor and delight that it overshadowed any flaw.

"There is nothing to do at Waring Manor, but sew and eat," Pamela informed her, with a small sigh of resignation.

The Dowager cleared her throat, and Pamela became aware of the diminutive figure at the head of the table.

"Great-aunt Ambrosia!" she cried, and flung her arms around that muttering individual.

The Dowager raised her eyeglass. "Peagoose! That dress won't do, you know. We'll be busy creating an entirely new wardrobe for you before you may show your face in society."

"You haven't changed a bit, Lady Bowen—ready to chew my head off in a trice."

"Sit down, gel, and don't flit about so. It gives me a headache. That new velvet trim on your gown doesn't fool me for a moment. Elfina always was a nipfarthing when it came to spending money on anyone but herself." She pinched the material derisively.

"Don't embarrass Pamela the moment she steps into your presence," Amanda admonished with little effect.

Pamela giggled. "Don't worry, Mandy, I don't mind Great-aunt Ambrosia's blustering voice. Life wouldn't be the same without it." She sent the old woman a fond look.

"You always had a pretty turn of phrase, Pam. But you don't need to give me that blarney. I've already decided to make a handsome settlement on you in the advent of your marriage. I only hope Elfina will be alive to see it, as I would dearly enjoy watching her long face when I dish out the blunt." The Dowager wrung her gnarled hands in anticipation.

"Pam, Grandmama is set on marrying you off to some suitable young gentleman this season," Amanda warned.

"Oh?" Lady Pamela's fresh round face showed a trace of discomfort, and she repeatedly curled the corner of her napkin.

The Dowager made a calming gesture. "Don't fly into a pelter about it. Amanda will be doing the exact same thing—marrying, I mean, even if it is to that fleshmountain, Sir Digby."

Amanda shivered, squarely meeting her grandmother's frosty eye. "Luckily I am of age, Grandmama," she reminded her relative. "You cannot force me to wed anyone."

"Ha! What does that signify? If you don't marry, what will you do—and where will you go? To Bowen House in Berkley Square? You were happy enough to move in here when I offered. Yes, you came like you had fire in your petticoats," the Dowager crowed triumphantly.

Amanda's delicate features reddened. "You're becoming a complete despot, Grandmama. Worse every day."

The Dowager snorted. "I was only bamming. With my assistance you'll both be riveted, or at least betrothed by the end of the season. And don't you turn up your nose at Sir Digby, Mandy. He's quite a catch, even with that appendage of flesh around his middle."

"In all likelihood, he sent the flowers to the wrong house."

"Flowers? What flowers?" Lady Pamela's eyes grew round.

Amanda told her about the bouquet while taking silent note of Pamela's too-severe bun of chestnut hair, the long eyelashes, the glowing cheeks framing a rosebud mouth, and the long neck. Although several inches taller than Amanda, Pamela still gave the impression of soft petite femininity with her rather large bosom. Her sweetness of expression would bring the gentlemen to her feet.

"All this to-do positively frightens me, and I don't know how I'll ever manage to stand up on a dance floor with everyone staring at me," Pamela breathed.

"Didn't I tell you, Mandy, that she's a peagoose?" the Dowager said. "At the end of the season, I'll be left with two rejected harpies to make my life miserable."

"Don't pay any heed to Grandmama," Amanda said to comfort her friend. "I'll take you to my room and show you the latest fashion plates. The new patterns are ravishing."

"The wardrobe she needs will ruin me," the Dowager said petulantly, glowering from under half-closed eyelids at the two young women.

Lady Pamela burst out laughing. "You're roasting me, Great-aunt Ambrosia, but you might as well stop right now, because you invited me here. You'll have to accept me the way I am."

"You'll do, peagoose—you'll do very well," the Dowager wheezed between chuckles. With those words she rose with difficulty, and clutching her cane, she ambled out of the room.

"Odious," Amanda whispered.

"Phew, I know now what a fly feels under a magnifying glass," Pamela said with a weak smile.

"Strong men have been known to cower under Grandmama's eyes. It's the Bowen black look, you know. But I assure you, you passed muster."

Lady Pamela finished her breakfast and followed Amanda

to her bedchamber, where they spent several agreeable hours poring over the latest fashions.

They made a list of everything Pamela would need, and planned to set out that very afternoon to visit the milliners in Bond Street. Pamela donned one of Amanda's walking costumes and a pair of her slippers. Wearing straw poke bonnets embellished with satin ribbons, and accompanied by Meg, the ladies set forth in the Dowager's ancient barouche.

The spring wind wafted its soothing balm on their cheeks, and in the trees lining the streets, birds sang and bickered. Carriages crowded the cobblestone streets and footmen in bright liveries darted among the pedestrians carrying messages. A lady and her maid were walking a lapdog that barked at every passing vehicle.

Hill Street widened into Berkley Square, and the sunlight played on the light facades of the buildings.

Amanda pointed out the mansion where her father and Lurlene resided, and Gunters, the confectioner, on the opposite side. She promised Pamela they would stop on the way home for a taste of their delectable ices.

The next few days flew by in much of the same vein, and between fittings, Amanda took her friend to see the Elgin Marbles—Greek sculptures that Lord Elgin had shipped to England in 1803, and the wild animals at the Exeter 'Change in the Strand. They visited Hookham's library and the horseback spectacles at Astley's.

By the time Pamela had spent two exciting weeks in London, most of her new gowns had been created and delivered at the door in South Street. The top of her armoire was piled high with hat and shoe boxes, and the interior displayed a wide array of ball gowns, walking costumes, morning and afternoon dresses, spencers and pelisses.

Creating a new wardrobe for Lady Pamela wasn't Amanda's

only excitement over those weeks. She watched with mounting puzzlement as Sir Digby's daily bouquets of fragrant roses filled all the vases in the house. She was at a loss to understand why he hadn't come to pay her a morning call. Impatiently she awaited the moment when she could tell him in no uncertain terms that his affection and money were wasted on her.

And worse, the Dowager looked more and more thoughtful as each bouquet arrived. This, Amanda was sure, meant that her mind was busy devising strategies to bring about Sir Digby's speedy proposal of marriage!

Sir Digby, in his lair on St. James's Street, had been attacked by a sudden bout of nerves. He had heard of Amanda's row with Lord Saville at the Opera House, and as he was sensitive to every form of disruption, he wondered at the soundness of Saville's choice of bridal candidate.

Listless, he fortified himself with a chocolate éclair from a silver salver while eyeing his nephew, who stood by the window, with suspicion.

"Are you sure Miss Bowen will be present at the Duchess of Devonshire's ball tomorrow night?" Sir Digby asked in a tired voice.

"I have told you three times that Lurlene informed me—well, *complained* that her stepdaughter was going to make the evening miserable by her presence. Lurlene doesn't like to play the role of chaperone. Says it makes her appear old."

"Are you still pursuing that bird-witted female?" Sir Digby demanded. "I thought you had more sense than that, nevvy. I've never known you to act like a complete imbecile before. But I suppose a besotted heart can make a fool of any man. Sooner or later, you'll be given the reckoning."

He sounded so gloomy that Lord Saville gave a whoop of mirth.

"Blue-deviled, are you?" He inhaled a pinch of snuff from the gold oval box in his hand. "Would it make you feel better to dine in style at White's, open a few bottles of claret, and then participate in some leisurely card game at Brooks's?"

"Hmm, you have a point. There is no better cure than a lovingly prepared dinner and friendly company to pull one out of the doldrums. I daresay you could use that sort of cure to relieve yourself of that canker-like infatuation for Lady Bowen." Sir Digby saw a mulish look set his nephew's jaw, and made a dismissing gesture with his pudgy hand. "You don't have my approval, and well you know it. Collect your wits, nevvy!"

Delicately wiping the chocolate from his fingers with a snowy napkin, Sir Digby continued, "You will need your cunning to bring me to the altar with Miss Amanda Bowen—who, by the way, is not the softspoken female you led me to believe. I heard all about your encounter at the Opera House. I must be queer in the attic to listen to you."

With those words he laboriously pushed himself from the comforts of his favorite chair and steered his steps toward the door, closely followed by a grim-faced Lord Saville. "I admit I judged Miss Bowen wrongly, Uncle. But you cannot stop your wooing now."

"I was committed after I sent that first bouquet, y'know, and now I wish to God I had never sent it!"

CHAPTER 4

THE BALLROOM at Devonshire House in Piccadilly blazed with the warm light cast by hundreds of candles set in the chandeliers. Excited small talk sibilated like a gentle wind through the vast room crowded with elegantly dressed and coiffed members of the *beau monde*. Costly jewels, tiaras and necklaces competed with the brilliance of the candle-light and heavy satins.

Amanda was sitting on a spider-legged gilt chair against the wall, forced to endure Lurlene's malicious gossip. Pretending to listen, she toyed with the tiny pearls embroidered in a row down the front of her ice-blue silk dress.

Since the Dowager rarely ventured out in the evening, except to indulge in an occasional card game, Lurlene had to step into the role of chaperone. Amanda closed her ears to her stepmother's chatter and her gaze darted repeatedly to the tall double doors admitting a continuous stream of guests into the ballroom. Her fingers clenched the ivory and chickenskin fan with unnecessary force, and her slippered foot rapped an impatient tattoo on the floor.

Sir Digby and Lord Saville were among the last guests to

arrive, and Amanda expelled an impatient breath as they joined the throng. Sir Digby waddled forward walrus-style, and Amanda's eyes slitted with suspicion when he lifted a quizzing glass and glanced around the room. Finally his alert blue gaze fell on her.

With as graceful a bow as his portly figure would allow, he acknowledged her presence, and she bowed her head minimally in response. He looked considerably ill at ease, his fingers curling tensely around the hem of his tight white waistcoat. He directed a rapid flow of comments to the marquess at his side, and Amanda wondered what he was saying. She wrenched her gaze away from her unwanted admirer, and was careful to avoid Lord Saville's green gaze, even though she was breathlessly aware of his presence.

When the first strains of music filled the air, Lord Saville nudged Sir Digby in the ribs. "Do it, old boy, this is the time to fix your interest with Miss Bowen. Sending her all those flowers, you have made a good impression already, and she'll be eager to accept your proposal."

"I don't know about that," Sir Digby said glumly, but obediently trudged across the floor to Amanda's side.

Couples were already forming a set of cotillions on the dance floor when he bowed in front of Amanda and Lurlene. Addressing the chaperone, he said, "I would like to have this dance with Miss Bowen, if available."

Lurlene tittered and looked at Amanda with contempt. "Nobody else has asked her."

A thin line of irritation etched between her ebony eyebrows, Amanda pretended to look at her dance card which held pitifully few names.

"I'd be honored," she said coolly, and held out her hand toward him. This would be the perfect time to ask him to cease his amorous endeavors.

As they moved to take their places in the set, Sir Digby

muttered, "I never dreamt it would come to this—dancing I mean. It ain't one of my stronger points." His face puckered with discomfort and he stopped short of the dance floor. "Ahem . . . d'you think we could sit this out? I fear I would crush your dainty feet."

Amanda nodded, a small smile curving her lips at the thought of Sir Digby plodding around the room to the tune of the music. His face already shone red with embarrassment.

"I'd like a glass of ratafia, if you'd be so kind as to fetch it for me," she said amiably.

"With pleasure!" Brimming with relief, he led her to a sofa in an alcove partly concealed by a huge vase of sweet-smelling yellow roses. With unusual alacrity he set about procuring a glass of the cordial for her, and returned a few moments later.

After taking a sip, she said, "I must take this opportunity to thank you for the lovely roses. These many days I've expected you to call on me at home."

He fidgeted and searched fruitlessly in his pockets for his snuffbox, having forgotten where he'd put it. Keith had said nothing about calls, he thought, his mind awhirl in agitation. "Calls? Ahem—yes—of course." He mopped his perspiring brow with a large handkerchief.

Amanda decided to help him out of his obvious misery. "I daresay you're not used to courting a lady." She smiled, her erstwhile impatience rapidly evaporating.

"No—yes, well, it's deuced taxing!" He heaved a mournful sigh. "Who would ever want to be saddled with a man like me?"

Amanda's laughter tinkled. "Indeed!" she teased him, but upon seeing his crestfallen face, she patted his arm gently with her fan. "Don't take on so. I was merely bamming you. 'Tis my sincere opinion that a lady could do much worse."

He brightened perceptibly. "Then you're not averse to my suit?"

"I don't say I approve of it—in fact, I have no desire to marry you or anyone else, and I fail to understand what gave you the idea that I would be a willing target for your admiration." Her eyes sparkled.

Demmed Saville! Sir Digby's preoccupied gaze dashed to the ceiling and he wished he could fly away into the blue sky painted on the plaster frescoes.

"Eh . . . well, I've always admired you, Miss Bowen." He took a deep noisy breath, rallying all his courage. "I'm useless at this kind of game, and might as well make a clean breast of it! You see, to claim the rest of my inheritance I have to marry." His face held a look of utter defeat. "You must despise me for trying my clumsy maneuvers on you, Miss Bowen. I swear it's easier to be raked over red-hot coals than to deal with females." Those last words he said with immense feeling.

"I see—and I would be the female in question?" Amanda was enjoying herself hugely.

"Well, I sincerely believe you'd be better than most, Miss Bowen. At least you're no simpering schoolmiss, and from what little I know of you, you appear to have a sensible head on your shoulders." That was mere conjecture, as he remembered with uneasiness her confrontation with Saville at the Opera. He stole a glance at her, taken aback at the amusement on her face. "You're laughing at me!"

"No such thing, Sir Digby. I'm flattered that you would consider me a likely candidate."

"Oh," came his lame response. He shrugged his massive shoulders and almost revealed that the idea had been Lord

Saville's. "I expected the most blistering of snubs. But I find I cannot live with the pretense of being your ardent admirer." Too late did he see the veiled insult. With a sheepish demeanor, he went on, "Er, what I mean—"

"Don't worry, Sir Digby. I appreciate your sincerity," Amanda said cordially. "And I couldn't stand to hear nauseating declarations of undying love, since we're not very well acquainted."

He pursed his lips. "You must take me for a regular shabster, Miss Bowen, but I assure you, this little talk has convinced me that you're a very reasonable female— contrary to recent rumors."

Her lips twitched. "It seems my behavior at the Opera House will dog me to the end of my days, but I'm glad that you have a flexible mind, Sir Digby."

They sat in companionable silence until Amanda snapped her fan shut. Sir Digby twisted his head sideways, almost stabbing his eye with the high shirtpoint, and looked at her with considerable trepidation.

"You won't let this little chat become public knowledge now?" he asked in a faint voice.

She glared at him with mock ferocity. "Of course not! Do you take me for a complete goosecap?"

"Not at all," he hastened to soothe her. "In fact, I believe you're up to all the rigs—if you excuse the cant expression."

Ignoring the prying eyes directed at them, Amanda gave a delightful ripple of laughter. "I'm sure Lord Saville doesn't share your tolerant opinion, but that's neither here nor there." She noticed a deep flush creeping up his fleshy jowls, and she wondered at the cause of his sudden discomfort. Thoughtfully she studied the rose pattern of the carpet.

"Are you really determined to find a wife this season, Sir Digby?"

He squirmed at her direct question. "Well, to tell you the truth, matrimony papers appear less and less desirable at this point—inheritance, or no inheritance." He plucked at the gold buttons of his waistcoat.

"Then we are in accord, because I'm of the same opinion. But I have a proposition that could be quite comfortable for both of us."

His eyes flew wide with surprise, and then slitted with suspicion.

"No, not *that* kind of proposition, Sir Digby. No, what I have in mind is quite innocent."

His fingers worked harder at his buttons and she continued, her mien unperturbed: "We could *pretend* that we've embarked on a romantic attachment, which would get Grandmama off my back." She paused for a moment, her brows knit together. "Hmm, but that wouldn't solve your dilemma."

Thinking of Lord Saville pushing him into this uncomfortable situation, Sir Digby responded with enthusiasm. "You know, that is a splendid scheme. It would give me a respite from a certain person pressuring me as well. I don't think I'm cut out for holy wedlock—at least not at this point. But I don't mind dancing attendance on such a—a *handsome* female as you," he blurted out recklessly, his face red.

Amanda almost stretched out her hand to shake his, as if concluding a bet, but recovered from the unladylike urge. Instead she fluttered her fan in front of her face. The air was hot and redolent with the scent of burning wax and the warm spice of cut flowers.

Feeling as if she had won a victory, she let her gaze travel around the room, and she was startled to find Lord Saville's steely eyes fixed upon her in speculation from across the floor. The room suddenly seemed suffocating and Amanda longed to escape onto the terrace to get away from him.

"Lord Saville is staring at me most rudely; I suppose he's planning some awful revenge for my conduct at the Opera," she said.

Sir Digby cleared his throat. "My nephew always had a fierce temper, but I'm positive he didn't pay any heed to your—er, insults."

Amanda had momentarily forgotten that Sir Digby and Lord Saville were close relations. Her voice at its driest, she said, "I daresay. He must be curious to know—like the rest of the assembly—what business has kept us in this alcove for more than half an hour. If Grandmother were here, she would send you away with a flea in your ear."

"Heaven forbid!" Sir Digby heaved himself ponderously out of the sofa. "I assume Saville has been making an idiot of himself at your stepmama's feet. I'd better escort you back to where she's holding court."

Amanda glanced at him with new interest. "You don't share the general adoration for Lurlene?"

Not daring to say something that would show his dislike of the lady in question, Sir Digby donned an inscrutable expression as he escorted Amanda across the gleaming parquet floor. Bowing, he inquired in a loud voice if he could take her for a ride in Hyde Park the following day, an invitation Amanda was delighted to accept.

Sir Digby betook himself out of the ballroom to settle down at a cardtable in the adjoining salon. Amanda was pleased with the outcome of their discussion, which would protect her—at least temporarily—from Grandmama's tiresome schemes.

Her pleasure was short-lived when Lord Saville joined the ever growing circle around Lurlene. He lingered just on the fringe, but to Amanda's surprise, his eyes were still trained on her, and not on the radiant object of his ardor. She bravely met his gaze, forming her countenance into a forbidding frown.

He wore full evening attire, satin knee-breeches and black tailcoat, a diamond winking in the immaculate folds of his neckcloth, his hair brushed to glossy waves.

"I beg your pardon, Miss Bowen. If looks could kill, I would definitely lie flat on the floor—gasping for my last breath." A diabolical smile played on his face. "It was my humble hope that you'd allow me this dance, if it isn't already spoken for?"

With incredible speed he snapped up the dance card dangling from a cord around Amanda's wrist. To her outrage, he scrawled his name on the appropriate line and said, "Now it is."

Speechlessly aware that the situation was slipping out of her control, she watched him take hold of her stiff fingers and pull her away from the crowd around Lurlene.

"Of all the arrogant—" she began.

"Shhh, spare your ammunition, Miss Bowen; perhaps it will come in handy later."

With a scorching stare, she had to give in to the subtle pressure of his fingers on her waist as he placed his arm around her in the waltz. Short of making an embarrassing scene, she couldn't escape his unwanted closeness.

She had to admit he was, despite his limp, a skillful dancer as he led her in forceful twirls around the floor. The spellbinding music caught her, softening her outrage, and she began to enjoy the sensation of being perfectly in tune with her dance partner. As if he had lifted her onto a downy cloud, she floated where nothing could touch her except the magic of the dance. His relentless arm secured her in that heady state of suspension, and as happiness suffused her being, she gazed into his hard face. His closeness and his virile scent seduced her senses, and he seemed so different, the smoky green of his eyes almost tender as he gazed into her hot face. An unbidden tingle of anticipation eddied through her, and the unyielding strength of his shoulder made her long to touch the curls at the nape of his neck. Her fingertips dug into the smooth fabric of his coat.

"I always thought your eyes were black, Miss Bowen, but I see that I was wrong—they are dark blue," he mused *sotto voce*, "with streaks of black velvet."

Dazed by the heated whisper of his breath on her face, Amanda let down her usual guard. "There was never any mistaking the smoky emerald of your eyes, milord." Her voice sounded so far away. Had she really breathed those sultry words?

She examined the faint lines around his eyes; the sable, almost feminine eyelashes with their upward tilt; the dangerous, wildly sensual lips that she suddenly yearned to kiss. His square stubborn chin brought her back to her senses.

Tongue-tied and increasingly flustered, she noticed the world around her, the designing eyes of the guests, the effervescent voices. For one moment panic seized her.

"And your hair is shot with blue lights—very unusual in a British lady."

"You have no business putting my coloration under such close scrutiny, milord," Amanda retorted with newfound aplomb. "You're forgetting your manners."

His arm gripped harder around her waist, and his lips took on a sarcastic curl. "Manners be condemned to a very hot place! I never took the time to look close before, but I see now that your eyes don't match your wicked tongue. Your tart speech hides well your passionate nature—but the eyes never lie, and if I weren't this close—"

"Milord! How dare you speak such shocking nonsense?"

He chuckled. "I'm sure you're well aware that I'm known as a blackguard who never follows the rules. You must be privy to all the sordid gossip about me."

Uncomfortable, Amanda wished the dance were over. Searching madly for a scathing remark to cover her confusion, she blurted out, "You must have a high opinion of yourself if you think that people have nothing to discuss but your conduct."

When that failed to provoke him, she added, "Besides, it's rude to surmise that I listen to gossip, Lord Saville."

He laughed, a soft enervating sound meant for her ears alone. "Saintliness doesn't suit you, Miss Bowen; everyone, without exception, partakes in gossip."

"I prefer to believe what I see," she retorted, attempting to wiggle out of his ever-tightening grip. "And if you're trying to embarrass me, I beg you to stop this very instant, because it fails to amuse me. What are you do—?"

Her head spun as he whisked her behind a potted palm shielding the open double doors leading to the terrace.

"Let go of me this instant!"

But before she had time to tear herself out of his grasp, he had whirled onto the terrace. They danced the whole length of the paved surface.

"Are you afraid, Miss Bowen?" His voice grated rawly on her senses. "After the annihilating rake-down you gave me at the Opera, I thought nothing could frighten you." His breath caressed her neck, sending feathers of excitement along her nerves.

"How dare you! Of all shabby conduct—this is—" Her voice trembled, revealing her agitation.

He let her go with a sudden twist, and leaned against the wrought-iron balustrade. "Well, are you going to rush back inside and complain to everyone about my scandalous behavior?"

Amanda got hold of her breath, her hands balled into fists at her sides, and her bosom swelling with wrath.

The pale moonlight showed the acerbic slant to his lips as he silently regarded her. "Well?"

The single word lay like a whiplash on her nerves.

"I think you're the most selfish, insolent creature alive! And if you take me for a peagoose ready to kiss the ground that you walk on, you're unbearably conceited."

She was badly shaken, but mostly from the passionate reaction he had provoked with his touch. Her skin still tingled from the memory. "Why don't you join Lurlene's court and leave me alone," she improvised.

"Ah! So you resent my amorous involvement with Lady Bowen." His low laughter teased her. "Perhaps I'll transfer my adoration to your feet. I'll kiss the very ground that *you* walk on—or perhaps those maddening lips." His features wreathed in a provocative smile, he seized her waist and pulled her hard against him. She was aware of every muscle pressing into her. His breath tempted the soft flesh of her lips. "They are the color of ripe cherries, and I like cherries very much."

Before Amanda knew what was happening to her, his mouth found hers, his tongue pressing through the barrier of her teeth with a power that sent a hot thrill curling over her skin. His arms cradled her securely against his lean body, and she had lost all willpower to push him away.

It startled her to find that she didn't want to. She secretly reveled in the feel of his well-knit body touching where no man had touched, and his intoxicating scent that forced her to betray her ladylike upbringing as she clung shamelessly, winding her fingers through the curls at his nape.

Lord Saville groaned softly when he finally let go of her

lips, and he breathed hard into her hair. "So fiery and so dulcet—those were by far the sweetest cherries I've ever tasted," he whispered.

She gathered her scattered wits. "I daresay that is an immense compliment coming from someone who must have tasted every sort of fruit."

"My dear Miss Bowen," he taunted, "you have a way of finding the most lowering of comments, but then you must be quite used to the ways of the world after so many seasons in London. I'm surprised that no gentleman has claimed you for himself."

His near-insulting statement revived her stunned temper. "That is none of your business, milord! And now if you please, unhand me before I call for assistance."

"Ah! Where would your reputation be then, Miss Bowen? You have now spent at least twenty minutes in the arms of a—top-lofty ignorant—or isn't that the exact title you gave me at the Opera House?"

"Ohhh, you—you—"

His voice turned icy soft. "Don't fly into the boughs, Miss Bowen. I'm startled to find such heady lips guarding such a careless tongue. I hope this has taught you the importance of relying more on that sweetness in the future."

"How dare you—" Amanda began, but was already addressing his back. "Blackguard!" she flung after him while her face flamed with humiliation and wrath. She yearned to box his ear. But he walked away, his uneven gait echoing along the stone terrace.

CHAPTER 5

"You idiot!" Lord Saville chided himself. "Did you have to go and ruin everything?" He was tearing off his evening attire, tossing his elegant tailcoat on the nearest chair in his bedchamber. Pushing a hand through his hair, he stared at his face in the mirror above the chest of drawers topped with a lint brush and a hair brush. He had aged since that fateful day with Lurlene, which wasn't a surprise, considering—

He swore and dragged off his shirt, almost losing his balance in the process. A stab of pain shot through his leg and he groaned. The ache forced perspiration to his forehead and he sank down on the edge of the bed. Rubbing his tortured shin, he realized he would have to live with this for the rest of his life. The knowledge forced tears of pain and hopelessness to his eyes.

Deep in thought, he paid no attention to the glory of the rising sun painting the sky orange above the jagged horizon of the London dwellings. He pulled off his breeches and stretched out in his bed. As he closed his eyes, the image of Amanda's outraged face swam before him.

Tonight he had almost ruined Dig's chances at connubial

bliss. "How could you do it?" he muttered to himself, wallowing in a sea of guilt. Why had he kissed Miss Bowen? Was it his retribution for the insult she had given him at the Opera—or something else, something he had not anticipated when he had studied her, the woman he had chosen to be Digby's bride?

And not only that, but he had danced. Since the injury in his leg, he never danced. Bitterness fought with sadness. He had never been quite the same since his leg broke. Tomorrow he would set about exacting payment for his pain. He had to, if he was ever going to feel at peace again. Desperation churned within him, as if he needed to avenge himself on the entire world.

He shook his head vigorously to clear away the ever-tightening black thoughts, then burrowed his head into the pillow and slept heavily for a few hours, oblivious to the rattling coach wheels and shouts in Grosvenor Square as the morning grew late.

Standing at the foot of the bed, Lumley, Saville's valet, coughed discreetly. "I believe 'tis time to shave, milord. I have heated the water."

The marquess aimed a bleary eye at his valet. "Already? I quite lost the track of time." He rose, stretched his stiff limbs, and entrusted himself to the care of the servant. A trickle of excitement coursed through him. He was finally going to do something about his pain. Today would be a new beginning.

An hour later, clean-shaven and invigorated by two cups of strong coffee, Lord Saville sallied forth. Savoring the dazzling spring sunlight, he ignored the stabs in his leg, and walked a few blocks. At the corner of Grosvenor Street and Bond Street he hailed a hackney to take him to Ludgate Hill, to the fashionable jewelers Rundell, Bridge and

Rundell, where he intended to set the first step of his scheme into motion.

Lacking the energy to tool his curricle around the park, Sir Digby collected Amanda in a landau on the afternoon following the ball. It was an open carriage with softly upholstered seats in which they could comfortably carry on a chat while the coachman did the driving.

At the fashionable hour of five o'clock, the sandy lanes of Hyde Park were crowded with barouches, curricles, broughams, and phaetons. Young bucks were showing off their high-stepping bits o' blood, adding to the general confusion.

As the day was unusually warm, the budding leaves were unfurling rapidly, draping the trees bordering the lanes in delicate green veils. The flowering tulips displayed an explosion of color, mostly red and yellow, and Amanda commented on the beauty of the park.

"Yes, I daresay spring is my favorite season," Sir Digby admitted. " 'Tis a rare pleasure to be abroad." He peered at her in appreciation. "I'm glad we've come to such a convenient understanding, Miss Bowen. It takes a heavy load from my shoulders." He patted his perspiring brow with his ubiquitous handkerchief.

"I agree, but—come to think of it—there is still a slight problem. How will our bargain help you gain your inheritance?"

He squirmed. "After examining my conscience carefully, I've come to the conclusion that I'd rather curb my expenses than become riveted for life to a lady who will spend her days trying to change my, er—eating habits." He patted his paunch gently. "I beg your pardon for my bluntness, but I want you to know the truth." Then his expression puckered with dismay. "I hope you haven't already changed your mind about our little arrangement."

A smile softened Amanda's features. "No, not at all. In fact, I most fervently insist that we continue in the same vein. I count on you to caress my hand and look besotted, especially in the presence of my grandmother, to convince her of your ardor. She's determined to wed me off this season, and I shudder to think what hapless gentleman she would foist on me." She chortled. "You and I are the only ones who will know the true state of affairs, of course. The charade will be easy to maintain, and you can trust me to jilt you at the end of the season."

His eyes widened with uneasiness at her frank words, but as she smiled, he instantly collected himself and waved languidly at a passing acquaintance. "The courtship's a deuced tedious business, but a very effective ruse. You have a devious mind, Miss Bowen." He looked almost frightened, as if doubting the merits of such a trait.

"I believe all people—even women—should use their brains, thereby creating a better world."

He stared at her in disbelief. "How very odd a sentiment, to be sure." They were the target of many curious glances from the passengers in passing vehicles, and the air was rife with speculation. Well aware of their audience, Amanda forced a continuous bright smile to her lips and she often leaned forward to pat Sir Digby's arm with her fan. He struggled to keep a besotted smile on his face, but repeatedly had to apply his handkerchief to his perspiring forehead.

Amanda wondered if she'd made a mistake by pushing the shy man into the subterfuge, but it was too late to stop now.

Her thoughts returned frequently to her confrontation with Lord Saville on the previous evening. The memory of his kiss nagged at her mind and made her heart race. The rhythmic sound of cantering horses, the happy creaking of springs, and the sunny afternoon could not banish the distress that had haunted her since Lord Saville had left her on the terrace of Devonshire House. Only her breeding prevented her from showing any of her inner turmoil.

"Grandmother is preparing a ball next week to bring out my dearest friend, Lady Pamela Waring, and I'll make sure that you get an invitation, Sir Digby." Recalling Pamela's fondness for food, she added, "I think you'll like her."

"I ain't much in the petticoat line, Miss Bowen—if you'll excuse my expression." Hot color crept over Sir Digby's collar. Amanda felt a twinge of pity for him, but the sentiment was rapidly swept away as a shadow—that wasn't her parasol—suddenly shielded her from the sun.

"Ah, Saville!" Sir Digby exclaimed with alacrity. His fleshy lips trembled in a relieved smile at being rescued from the frightening wasteland of polite conversation.

Amanda's gaze lit into the darkly handsome visage of her tormentor. Her heart hammered wildly, and the force of his gaze chased the breath from her lungs. To pay him back for his ruthless kiss at the ball, she wanted to snub him, to give him a scathing remark, but none left her tongue.

"Miss Bowen, I hope I find you in the best of health after the late evening at Devonshire House. I wager you didn't sit out one dance after I left," Saville said with a mocking bow. His stallion, a dappled gray, skittered sideways, dragging his master's green gaze momentarily away from Amanda. In the short time it took him to bring the animal under control, Amanda forced herself to calm down.

"I doubt you can take the credit for my departure from the wallflowers' row of chairs," she said, her voice frosty. She adjusted her parasol to conceal her face from his probing eyes.

Lord Saville laughed heartily. "I don't need the credit. I hope you enjoyed our waltz as much as I did."

Sir Digby looked from one to the other. "Did you dance with Miss Bowen last night, nevvy?" When Saville replied with a curt nod, he continued, "But you never take to the dance floor. Your—er—leg." His eyes were wide circles of surprise.

Amanda realized he had been pleased with his nephew's sudden appearance, but as animosity flowed thick between her and the marquess, Sir Digby's face displayed bewilderment.

A smile lingered at the corners of Lord Saville's lips. "I had to still my curiosity about Miss Bowen. You seemed to find her company vastly entertaining in the alcove at Devonshire House, Uncle."

Sir Digby fidgeted on his seat, clearing his throat violently as if the situation was growing too complicated to handle. "I did—I do," he muttered.

"I believe Lord Saville doesn't share your opinion, Sir Digby, but be that as it may," Amanda said in dismissing tones. Then she slanted a black look at Lord Saville. "And I fail to understand *your* sudden interest in my humble person."

Lord Saville chuckled, a sound of unexpected warmth. "Humble, Miss Bowen? I see no evidence of that admirable quality in your character."

"Has it ever occurred to you that there may be more than meets the eye?" she parried, her body still rigid with disapproval. She wasn't going to let his charm soften her. "It appears that your judgment is hasty at best."

"What an alarming thought. You're undermining my confidence." The smile still played on his face. "You must take me for a regular counter-coxcomb."

Amanda couldn't prevent her lips from bending upward,

her resistance reluctantly melting under the onslaught of his charm. "I didn't think you cared about my opinion."

"Curious, that's all." He stared at her through slitted eyelids.

"Counter-coxcomb? No. I think you are a . . . top-lofty ignorant," she said in smooth tones and hid her smile behind her fan.

"Your snub is wounding me mortally," he rejoined, placing a hand tragically to his heart.

"Nevvy, cease talking such gammon!" Sir Digby said irritably. He mopped his flaming countenance, throwing a series of nervous glances at Amanda's face.

The landau continued its sedate journey, Lord Saville's stallion effortlessly keeping abreast. The marquess looked splendid in a bottlegreen riding coat with large pewter buttons, white doeskin pantaloons, and Hessian boots. The brim of his tall beaver hat cast a shadow over the dangerous light in his eyes.

Sir Digby hailed Lord "Poodle" Byng, who was driving a perch phaeton, his poodle sitting on the seat beside him. As Sir Digby imperiously dug his cane into the coachman's back, the landau jerked to a halt. Obviously seeking solace from the churning tension between Amanda and Lord Saville, Sir Digby ponderously leaned over the side of the carriage to speak with his friend.

Lord Saville's gaze, meanwhile, rarely left Amanda's face, and she nervously squeezed the handle of her parasol.

"I feel a snub was quite in order," she murmured. "Your conduct at the ball was hardly gentlemanly, after all."

"I only acted in accord with my rakish character," he rejoined, his lips twitching irrepressibly. Noting her suspicion, he added, "Spare your vitriol, Miss Bowen—I'm merely roasting you."

"How very kind. If you believe you can shock me into

losing my temper, you think far too highly of yourself," she retorted with acid sweetness. "Besides, I don't believe for one minute that you're as bad as you pretend to be." Yet, in her thoughts she suspected the opposite.

He laughed dryly. "*Touché*, Miss Bowen. I admit that I expected you to cut me dead after last night's kiss."

"For a single kiss?" she said, carefully tinting her voice with contempt. An exquisite shiver pulsed through her. Never would she confess what havoc his kiss had done to her senses.

His glance was roguish, and she felt a twinge of unease. "I take it you're very experienced in the art of kissing, Miss Bowen?"

She prayed that the heat spreading over her entire body would not suffuse her face with red, but she prayed in vain. Averting her gaze, she murmured, "It's quite rude of you to suggest that I have such an easy virtue that I take pleasure in illicit kissing."

"I'm sure many admirers have been tempted when confronted by the sweet curve of your lips." His voice was low, a velvet caress on her senses. "As I was tempted last night."

"And you had to have your way with me? I don't think politeness or consideration is one of your stronger character traits," she argued. "A herd of *cattle* would have treated me more gently."

She thought he looked stung, and his next words confirmed her suspicion. "I see that I was right comparing your character to that of the Dowager Lady Bowen. Her legacy to you is evident—your ruthless frankness, which is perhaps a shade daunting in a young lady of quality."

"No one has ever complained before," she said, careful to keep her voice neutral. "Besides, I give as good as I get." Her heart beat so hard against her ribs that she was certain he could hear it. "And I don't recall asking for your opinion."

His face split into a grin. "At the moment, your lips are simply mulish. Did my comment touch you on the raw, Miss Bowen? Can't you take frank speech in return? After all, ever since our first meeting, we've always indulged in the truth, no matter how unsavory."

"I *do* like frank speech, but your words continuously stab me with hidden barbs."

"Ah! And yours don't?"

The words hung in the breathless air between them.

Amanda wanted to stab him with her umbrella. "I won't bother to answer that. I haven't the veriest desire to continue a conversation with a man whose sole aim it is to goad me and ruin this perfectly wonderful afternoon."

"I find our verbal sparring quite invigorating, Miss Bowen." His blazing smile made her heart lurch uncomfortably.

"You choose a victim to confront, then thrive on his or her discomfort? I'm not surprised." Her eyes felt hot with anger and she could barely remain calmly in her seat. "Is that why you have chosen to undermine my father's marriage to Lady Bowen?"

Suddenly it was hard to believe that a smile had ever softened Lord Saville's features as his face darkened dangerously. "You're a righteous little baggage, aren't you?" His voice was flat with anger. "It's obvious you don't know the first thing about my relation with Lady Bowen, so spare me your starchy lectures. And if you can't take a bit of banter, I foresee that your future will be bleak indeed."

With those words he pulled in the reins and tooled the stallion around in a neat circle, his begloved hands curling savagely around the leather. "Good-bye, Miss Bowen."

"Rudesby!" she called after him, her voice choking. She

pressed a lacy handkerchief to her lips in distress, and struggled to recapture her composure. How she had harped! The soft-spoken decorum of a true lady had slipped from her as soon as his shadow had fallen upon her. And he! He was a—a *devil*.

With a last hooded glance over his shoulder, Lord Saville tore off down the lane, his horse kicking up puffs of dust.

Closing her ears to the diminishing echo of the stallion's hoofs, Amanda swallowed hard, battling the angry tears clouding her sight. She pressed a hand over her thundering heart. Her mind barely registered that the landau was moving.

"Good God! What did my nephew say to bring such distress to your lovely eyes, Miss Amanda?" Sir Digby asked, peering at her with genuine compassion. He clenched and unclenched his hands. "If he were here, I'd knock him down."

Amanda smiled weakly. "We were only quibbling. It doesn't signify in the least."

"Lord Saville always had a wicked tongue and a blazing temper. I've always warned him to be more careful—dashes about as if he has fire in his tailcoat, not caring who he cuts up," Sir Digby muttered. "I'll have him apologize to you."

Amanda glanced at her new friend's angry countenance. "Don't fret over it, Sir Digby. I confess our confrontation was partly my fault. I accused him of coming between my father and Lady Bowen." With a sigh, she confided, "I don't know why I can't hold my tongue. Lord Saville properly put me in my place, as his doings are none of my business."

Sir Digby grumbled unintelligibly into his extravagant neckcloth, his color very high as the last of the afternoon sunlight beat down on his tall hat. "I have many times spoken with him about that havey-cavey business with your stepmother, but he listens to no one. He has never told me why she jilted him. Don't fret about it, Miss Amanda. I'm sure your father is man enough to keep my nephew at bay."

She listened to him, wanting to believe his words. Yet she could not help but worry about her gentle father and that Lurlene would break his heart with the help of the heartless Lord Saville. "I pray you're right, Sir Digby."

His voice lower, he continued, "I daresay you won't believe me when I say that under all that haughty irony, Saville is a very decent fellow. But few have seen that side, of course. He has become worse since Lurlene broke their betrothal." Sir Digby fidgeted with his cuffs, clearly embarrassed mentioning family problems to her.

"He has yet to show me any facet of decency, Sir Digby, and frankly, I don't care if he never does. But let us enjoy what's left of this lovely afternoon."

"Yes, of course. Nevertheless, I'll make sure he doesn't attend Lady Pamela's come-out ball. I take it your stepmother will be present?"

"Naturally. Honestly, Sir Digby, you don't have to worry that I can't hold my own against Lord Saville."

Noticing that her reassurances made Sir Digby relax, Amanda patted his hand. She ignored the knot of anguish the confrontation with Lord Saville had left in the pit of her stomach, and gave her gallant companion a brittle smile.

CHAPTER 6

ONE OF THE DOWAGER Lady Bowen's best traits was her generosity to her family. For its members nothing was good enough. She had already heaped Lady Pamela with all the luxurious necessities for a successful first season, except the come-out ball. She had decided that Pamela's debut was going to make all other balls of the season pall by comparison.

There was but one problem to overcome. The Dowager's house in South Street, a handsome dwelling with sculptured plaster ceilings, plastered walls, and tall narrow windows, had no room large enough for the hundreds of guests she had planned to invite.

Pamela demurred, insisting that the ball need not be the greatest squeeze of the season, and that she was quite content with a smaller affair. But the Dowager would hear none of it.

"There is only one thing to do, however much I loathe the idea," she mused out loud at the breakfast table. "My teeth positively *ache* at the thought."

"What has put you in high fidgets this morning, Grandmama?" Amanda asked, calmly buttering her toast as she exchanged secret knowing glances with Pamela.

"Don't play the innocent with me, miss. You know very well that I'm planning Pamela's ball this morning, like I have been every waking moment for the last four weeks." The Dowager formed her lips into a down-turned crescent. "The problem is, we don't have a ballroom here."

Amanda chuckled. "How could I avoid noticing? You've hardly talked about anything else all week. You'll have to bow to the inevitable, and ask Lurlene's permission to use the ballroom at Berkley Square."

"Don't speak that *name* in my presence." The Dowager's face contorted, giving it the look of a dry apple. She expelled a sigh of heavy disgust, a sure sign of her defeat. "Very well, we might as well get it over with. We'll pay *her* a visit this morning."

An hour later the three ladies set forth in the Dowager's ancient barouche for the short ride to Berkley Square. It was a blustery and overcast day, the air invigorating and filled with the scent of rain. The carriage turned onto Hill Street and almost collided with a wagon stacked with barrels. The barouche swayed alarmingly and the coachman swore. Amanda looked out the window to see if any damage had occurred to the other vehicle, but it rattled past, its driver shaking a knotted fist at the Dowager's coachman.

Amanda saw a grimy urchin pushing a wheelbarrow filled with fish, and a baker was carrying a tray of pastries. A flower girl offered a bouquet of red tulips at a street corner, and a small boy in nankeen breeches and a brown coat was playing with a puppy.

"What are you doing, gel, hanging out the window like a common trollop?"

"Nothing, Grandmama, I was looking at the people on the street."

"Too nosy for your own good," grumbled the Dowager. She resembled a tiny bird in her gray taffeta gown that had been fashionable twenty years before. Plumes nodded in her turban, and a pair of hideous gold earrings in the shape of lion heads adorned her ears. Amanda wore a morning gown of green-striped muslin with a matching pale green pelisse. Pamela's glowing complexion rivaled her pink outfit as she contemplated the upcoming ball. "I'm so very grateful, Great-aunt Ambrosia, that you would go through all the trouble of a ball for me," she said with a timid smile.

The Dowager looked askance. "Silly goose. This is the only thing I have left—don't you see? I cannot dance any longer, but I still have enough power to sit like a spider in my web and pull the strings. Mark my words, your come-out will be quite as extravagant as Amanda's was four years ago. Even though it was quite wasted on *her*. She hasn't been able to make any gentleman come up to scratch despite all the expenditures lavished on her over the years."

Amanda tossed her curls. "If you're trying to make me feel guilty, it won't work." She pretended a sudden interest in the houses they passed, while pincers of guilt twisted her insides. "You're a tyrant, Grandmama."

"And where would you be without me, pray? Waiting hand and foot on *that woman!* I know there is nothing wrong with your wit, but you're much too dispassionate about your future, Mandy."

Amanda smiled wryly at her grandmother's words, recalling yesterday's verbal battle with Lord Saville. She was coming to realize that if she went about finding a husband using that strategy, she would have to resign herself to a life of loneliness. Yet, without love, she'd rather stay unmarried. To direct her grandmother into more positive thoughts about her future, Amanda played her only trump card.

"I do have Sir Digby sitting in my pocket. By the way,

you shan't forget to send him an invitation to the ball, Grandmama?"

"Ha! That fleshmountain." The Dowager fidgeted with the buttons of her gray kid glove. "But I suppose for all that flesh, he's not a bad suitor—not bad at all. Nevertheless, he's not quite what I had *foreseen* for you, Mandy. You need someone who can appreciate *all* your qualities, not just the fact that you're an eligible female. 'Tis especially important now when blond hair and blue eyes are all the rage." She stared critically at Amanda's mahogany curls peeking out of her poke bonnet.

Amanda was spared the trouble of answering as the barouche pulled up at the imposing black front door of the Bowen mansion in Berkley Square.

Mr. Lipton, the Bowens' stately butler, met them in the hallway.

"Good morning, Lipton," the Dowager said, jabbing her cane impatiently on the checkered marble floor of the foyer.

The old butler smiled warmly at Amanda as he escorted them to the morning room on the second floor. Amanda returned her old friend's smile. She had known Lipton all her life; he had always given her special treats from the kitchen when she was unhappy, and he had always been willing to listen to her woes.

As Lipton opened the door to the morning room, Amanda saw that Lurlene was holding sway over a retinue of gentleman callers.

"The Dowager Lady Bowen, Miss Bowen, and Lady Pamela Waring," Lipton announced in important tones. He then glided out of the room, closing the door softly behind him.

Lurlene surged forward, the frothy lace edging of her white and pink striped lawn gown accentuating her graceful movement.

"*Dearest* Mama," she gushed, slim hands outstretched in a theatrical welcome.

"Don't try to pull the wool over my eyes, Lurlene. You can't stand me any more than I can stand you, so don't give me that blarney." The Dowager raised her quizzing glass to survey the other occupants of the room, and the young— and not so young—gentlemen cringed in turn under the Bowen black look.

"I have something very important to discuss with you, Lurlene," she said pointedly, and the gentlemen immediately began to move, awkwardly pushing their chairs back.

Lurlene noticed the commotion. "You don't have to send away my guests, Mama," she exclaimed peevishly. "I'm sure we can speak privately for a few minutes in the rose salon."

The Dowager gave her daughter-in-law an affronted toss of plumes. She motioned toward Amanda and Pamela, who struggled to keep their faces serious. "And leave these two innocents to be fawned upon by this lot of toadeaters? Upon my dead body."

Two red spots appeared on Lurlene's cheeks. "Very well." She motioned carelessly for the trio of ladies to sit down. The Dowager purposely aimed her steps toward a chair occupied by a young sprig of fashion, whom she gave a look of burning disapproval. He rose awkwardly and sidled toward the door. The other gentlemen took his cue and waved a perfunctory farewell to their "Goddess," and filed out of the room.

"You may serve me a glass of negus, Lurlene—and don't get upon your high horse about the loss of your admirers. No doubt they'll be back posthaste. Family matters come first, after all." Her gaze toured the luxuriously appointed salon, its golden moldings and panels of cream brocade, its paintings in gilt frames and Chippendale tables and chairs.

"Where are my Dresden figurines that used to stand on the mantelpiece, and my mother's brass collection?" When no answer was forthcoming, the Dowager added, "And where is my moonling of a son when he should be keeping an eye on you?"

Lurlene bridled, and Amanda had to hide her smile in her handkerchief. "Justin trusts me implicitly, and it's quite *comme il faut* to entertain gentlemen guests—why, in your youth, they were even allowed into the bedchamber during the morning toilette," Lurlene defended herself.

The Dowager donned a mask of frosty disapproval. "It all depends on one's *designs*. Are yours innocent, I wonder?"

"Grandmama, you might as well come to the point of our visit, as dagger-drawing won't accomplish anything. You don't want to provoke Lurlene's ire by insulting her in her own home," Amanda warned.

The famous Bowen black look bore down on Amanda's smiling countenance.

"Minx!" the Dowager said with an audible sniff and shifted in her chair. "Very well, we—er, I have come to beg a favor of you, Lurlene. To warn you, just in case you plan to be difficult, I won't accept a refusal."

Lurlene bristled up in anger, but checked her tongue with obvious effort. "I see. What can I do for you?" she asked, her eyes coldly alive with speculation.

The Dowager straightened her back to accentuate her authority. "Before I go on, let me remind you that this is rightfully my house, and that I—only out of foolishness—entrusted it to your dubious care."

"Grandmama!" Amanda admonished sharply, thinking the Dowager was going too far.

The Dowager coughed and fidgeted, clearly ill at ease. "Hrmph, we would like you to open up the ballroom for Pamela's ball, Lurlene; I will stand for the cost, perhaps even furnish you with a handsome new gown, although I'm well aware that your wardrobes literally *bulge* with fripperies."

Silence fell, thick with animosity as Lurlene launched a staring contest with the Dowager, which she was doomed to lose.

"Remember, you will reap all the glory as a hostess of the ball if you have it here," the Dowager pointed out.

That detail clearly made Lurlene view the issue more favorably, and she nodded archly. "I see your predicament, and I believe Pamela deserves to be brought out from a proper house—and what could be better than mine?" Bestowing on Pamela a lofty smile, she added, "You should do well sponsored by me. My connections are vastly important."

Lady Pamela smiled and nodded, her eyes misting with excitement. "I'm certain it will be the best ball of the season. Much too grand for me."

Amanda noticed a dangerous purple tinge invading the Dowager's face, so she hastened to intervene. "Nonsense! I'm happy it's settled then. Lurlene, aren't you going to tell Grandmama your happy news?" Disgusted with the important air on Lurlene's face, Amanda played impatiently with the silk tassel of her fan. "I haven't breathed a word since I thought you wanted to tell your good news yourself."

"Of course." Lurlene addressed the Dowager. "Since I'm in a delicate condition, nothing could persuade me to execute the details of a ball. You'll have to take care of all the preparations"—she tapped one calculating finger on the armrest of her chair—"except for the planning of the decor."

The Dowager's eyes almost popped. "Condition?" she gasped. As if the room had become airless, she fanned herself wildly, her lips pursing. "Well, that is some news!

Imagine, Justin a father again . . . when he should be a
grandfather."

Amanda laughed. "He isn't in his dotage, and I'm
looking forward to having a small brother or sister," she
said bravely, although that wave of agitation she always
experienced in Lurlene's presence was washing through her.

"Twaddle," the Dowager sputtered, for once without a
scathing comment.

Before Lurlene could take offense, Amanda decided to
turn the conversation back to the ball. "I believe Pamela
should have some say about the decorations; it's her ball,
after all."

"I'm sure I don't know the first thing—" breathed
Pamela.

"But it's *my* house," Lurlene said, in a tone that evidently
raised the Dowager's hackles.

The old woman opened and closed her mouth several
times, and Amanda knew that she was about to remind
Lurlene once again about the true ownership of the Berkley
Square mansion. No words came over her lips. Although
she still looked dazed at the prospect of another grandchild,
Amanda could see the wheels of her mind turning.

"Whatever Lurlene decides will be fine. I don't want to
cause an argument. You have all been very kind to me,"
Lady Pamela piped.

"Perhaps we can broach the subject at another time,"
Amanda suggested. "At least we can send out the invita-
tions now. Grandmama, are you ready to go?"

There was a knock on the door and Lipton announced
three gentleman callers, one of them Sir Anthony Fanshawe, a young pimply fop with a nonexistent chin who had
publicly sworn to love Lurlene eternally. The other two
gentlemen Amanda didn't know.

When seeing the Dowager, the gentlemen uneasily took

seats close to Lurlene. Shortly after the introductions, the talk reluctantly shifted to current gossip. Then Lipton returned and announced the next caller. "The Marquess of Saville."

CHAPTER 7

"Ah! Good morning—all," Lord Saville greeted.

Amanda drew a ragged breath and held it as long as it took him to enter. As the Dowager had before him, he raised his eyeglass to study the assembly. He looked the epitome of a town beau in a dark blue coat with the stamp of Weston written in the elegant cut, pale biscuit-colored trousers, Hessians polished to a mirror-like sheen, and a cravat tied in the Mathematical style. Amanda found herself thinking that his tousled jet-hued curls invited a caress. The thought made her inexplicably angry.

"Egad, at last I find you without your usual vast retinue of popinjays, Lurlene." He ignored all the men except Sir Anthony, whom he acknowledged with a curt nod. He bent for a long moment over Lurlene's hand, his fingertips playing with her rings. She gave him a blinding smile as he slowly straightened. An enigmatic expression darkened his eyes, and his lips curled faintly. "A relief indeed to find you available . . . Lurlene." As he spoke, his gaze roamed lazily. His surprise was feigned as he noticed the Dowager. "But who do we have here? By Jupiter! The Dowager Lady

Bowen . . . Miss Bowen, and an unknown beauty." He made an exaggerated leg in front of the Dowager, who reacted by pulling her eyebrows into a tight scowl.

"The crowd that just left merely made room for chawbacons like you, Saville. And your paying respects to Lurlene, most likely on the flimsiest of pretexts, is only more evidence that your mind has gone a-begging."

The marquess raised his eyebrows in appreciation of the old lady's repartee. "Haven't lost your touch, Lady Bowen—as full of vinegar as always, and just as surely the reason for the flight of Lurlene's admirers." He turned to Lady Pamela, dazzling her with his smile. "Lurlene, I'm burning with curiosity. Introduce me, I beg."

Lurlene fulfilled his request with obvious reluctance, resenting to play second violin to the pretty girl fresh from the country. Lord Saville turned on his full charm as he bent to kiss Lady Pamela's hand, and she looked positively stunned.

Amanda seethed in silence. She longed to say something that would abolish the exaggerated grin from his lips. Her cheeks grew hot. Dragging her gaze from Lord Saville's face, she implored her grandmother with a gesture to leave, which the old woman ignored, doubtlessly looking forward to half an hour of verbal sparring with the odious marquess.

Amanda's attention irresistibly returned to Lord Saville. His smirk was completely gone as he gave her a parody of a bow.

"Miss Bowen," he murmured. "My soul is still burning after the whiplash of your tongue in the park." To Amanda's surprise he chose to sit on the sofa next to her, which provoked a venomous glare from Lurlene.

"I seriously doubt that you have a soul, milord," Amanda said *sotto voce*.

"I pray I'm not interrupting some important family business," he said blandly to the hostess.

Lurlene favored him with an indulgent smile. "It's no secret," she said importantly. "I'm going to sponsor Lady Pamela's come-out ball."

The Dowager snorted.

Lurlene continued, "You're certain to receive an invitation, Keith, even though I know how tedious you find the *bon ton* parties. But this will be very special since I'm going to plan the decor myself."

That overbearing announcement was too much for Amanda, whose sensibilities were deeply shaken by Lord Saville's proximity. "Surely Lord Saville has no interest in ballroom decorations," she said. She slanted a molten glare in his direction, and thought she saw a flicker of wry understanding, but it was instantly gone as he drawled:

"With you at the helm, Lurlene, the squeeze is destined to be superior. Why, your presence is all the ornament needed to make any occasion a success."

"Farradiddle!" the Dowager grunted, her patience at an end. "I've never heard a more nauseating piece of flummery!"

"What would you have me say, Lady Bowen—that it will be a complete failure?" Lord Saville asked in bored tones.

"I say, Saville, that's the outside of enough!" Sir Anthony Fanshawe exclaimed.

Lord Saville shrugged with supreme indifference, and a hiss of outrage went through his rivals. Sir Anthony, to smooth the ruffled waves, engaged Lurlene and Lady Bowen in conversation.

To Amanda's dismay Lord Saville inched closer and murmured in her ear, "I'm fully expecting you to give me the rough side of your tongue in the Dowager's defense,

Miss Bowen." The smile in his voice completely unsettled her. "Go on, I'm waiting."

"I don't know if I'm on speaking terms with you, Lord Saville," she said coldly, and her gaze strayed to the tall window which was swathed in gold-colored draperies.

"What a frightening thought! You're mortifying me."

"Are you roasting me, milord?"

His eyes were mercurial under the half-closed eyelids. "Perhaps—a most diverting pastime since you're so touchy."

Amanda's black look, which wasn't as intimidating as that of the Dowager, bore down on his amused face. "Really? I thought dogging Lurlene was one of your favorite pastimes—a flick of her eyelash the coveted reward."

His face serious for a brief moment, he whispered, "Miss Bowen, you don't have to worry. I'm not about to launch some lurid attack on Lurlene here in broad daylight." He stared at her, his gaze one of the top-lofty variety. "And I don't meddle in your affairs. I suspect that you're sorely jealous of Lurlene's accomplishments."

Why did he always manage to pull out the worst in her? "A common human flaw, surely," she said, making her voice airy.

"Miss Bowen, you're not the little harmless mouse I thought at first—much more than that." He kneaded his chin thoughtfully. "I offer you an olive branch. We cannot always be bickering if you're going to be part of my family."

Amanda gasped. "What do you mean?"

He studied her idly. "Why, your involvement with my uncle, Sir Digby. I'm convinced you'll suit very well."

"Involvement? Er—well. It isn't supposed to be public knowledge," she hedged. In a single stark moment, she regretted her pact with Sir Digby. "Besides, it's no business of yours—and a ride in the park doesn't spell *involvement*."

"But your besotted glances give you away. You could do much worse," he said coolly, and hauled out his snuffbox with maddening slowness. "Digby is a very good man, and he would be hurt if you're merely playing with him." His gaze probed the depth of her soul, and she had to look away. What would he say—and do—if he found out about her charade with Sir Digby?

He continued, "Let me give you one piece of advice; never tell him to curb his appetite. He lives in constant fear that his future wife will force him to eat only bread and water."

Amanda couldn't stop a smile from leaping to her face. "I assure you, I don't need your advice. I have no intention of changing Sir Digby's eating habits as they are of no concern to me, and I don't know how we got onto this . . . delicate subject in the first place."

"I must be a severe trial to you, Miss Bowen, always rubbing you the wrong way."

"When you're assailed by such strange notions as you are today. I wish you wouldn't mingle in my affairs. Besides, Sir Digby has not proposed to me yet."

"I'll bet you a monkey that you'll be riveted to Sir Digby by the end of the season, Miss Bowen," he said in cajoling tones, a devil dancing in his eyes.

"Lord Saville—your language," she admonished, but her lips twitched appreciatively. "As a rule I don't wager, but I know it's a common habit among the gentlemen, a very silly one at that."

"I have the strongest suspicion that you don't hold us gentlemen in high esteem," he goaded softly, but Amanda was not to be roused. A challenging gleam shone in her eyes, and she had for one breathless moment forgotten her antagonism as they fenced.

"I believe gentlemen are a necessary evil."

A laugh rumbled in his chest. "Well! If that doesn't beat the Dutch." While donning a subtle expression of dismay, he expertly flicked open the snuffbox lid with his thumbnail. "Here I sit, like a great blabbering fool, opening myself up to the harsh scrutiny of a misanthrope."

"Balderdash! I don't hear any deep revelations, only phrases designed to taunt me," Amanda said pertly.

"Why, my dear Miss Bowen! You give me the blackest of characters."

"And you fully deserve it, milord. Your manners leave a lot to be desired—not to mention your conversation." Amanda tossed her head for emphasis, her curls bouncing.

His lazy grin made her knees turn into jelly. "In other words, I'm the most selfish, disobliging creature alive."

"Just so." A gurgle of laughter surged from her lips. "A regular shabster."

"Miss Bowen, your rake-downs give me mortal injuries. I beg of you, have some mercy." His strong fingers deliberately caressed the shining lid of his snuffbox, and Amanda found herself wishing to be on the receiving end of that touch.

She felt a stab of disappointment when their badinage was cut short by the Dowager's imperative voice.

"Girls, it's high time we take our leave." She rose, her old back rodlike with disapproval. Lady Pamela was dazed from listening to one gentleman's graceful compliments, so Amanda nudged her into action. She exchanged a last veiled glance with Lord Saville, whose face still bore the imprint of devilment. "Good-bye, little misanthrope," he flung gently after her, and chuckled as she hurried away.

Lurlene couldn't disguise her pleasure at their departure, which meant she would have a few moments to flirt with the marquess. But this expectation was immediately squashed

as the Dowager commanded her in quelling tones to escort
them downstairs, since she had a few more words to say in
private.

Amanda's blood sang wildly in her veins as she descended the curved staircase behind the Dowager. All the
colors appeared more vivid, the sun emerging from behind
the clouds, more golden. And the grind of squeaky carriage
wheels and shouts from street vendors outside were music
to her ears. She barely noticed her grandmother giving her
a long measuring look.

While awaiting her grandmother, she fled outside with
Pamela in tow. "Let's buy a pastry at Gunters'," she said,
and Pamela agreed readily.

"I haven't stopped gaining weight since I arrived in
London," she said as they crossed the square. "There are
too many delicacies to sample, but if I'm not careful, my
gowns will be too small before the end of the season."

"Nonsense," Amanda said, and stepped into the shop.
The air was redolent with the scent of freshly baked bread.
They sat down at one of the tables, Amanda ordered a
raspberry tart, Pamela a plate of chocolate éclairs which she
began eating rapturously as soon as they arrived.

"The marquess is awfully handsome," she said between
bites.

A twinge went through Amanda's heart. "He's evil."

Pamela laughed, holding a napkin to her lips.

"Evil? Dangerous, perhaps, but not evil. I believe he's
quite taken with you. He gave you these long, enigmatic
looks."

Amanda smiled grimly. "He was trying to stab me to
death with them." She rose, swallowing the last of the tart.
"There's Grandmama now."

Pamela pushed the remains of the last éclair into her
mouth and followed Amanda outside.

Back in South Street, Pamela could talk of nothing but the upcoming ball. Amanda listened with mixed feelings as they discarded their bonnets and readjusted their curls after the visit to Berkley Square.

"I wish I had some of your calm assurance, Mandy," Pamela confided with a sigh. "Unfortunately I'm the veritable country bumpkin. This is all so new—I feel as if I've stepped into a fairy tale."

Amanda gave her friend a kind smile. "You'll be familiar with the way of polite society soon enough. My calmness is feigned, I assure you. And I feel a trifle bored with the rounds of balls and routs."

"Really?" Pamela gasped. "How can you be bored? I've never been so excited in my life."

"You forget that I've lived in London for four years, Pam, and there isn't much I haven't seen or heard. One tends to get disillusioned—and worn to a shade. After a while, the balls are all alike, and one always has to worry about clothes and coiffures. I'm ready for a new phase where the latest fashions aren't the hub of my life." She sighed. "Perhaps I should take up another hobby besides reading."

Pamela's mouth formed a round O, but nothing could squelch her newfound pleasure. This was her first season, and, by Jove, she was going to enjoy it to the fullest.

"You should try living with my grandmother at Waring Manor," she said with a giggle. "That would bring you back to town posthaste in a different frame of mind. She will not allow you to read the latest books. You're doomed to reading the Bible or being chained to the embroidery frame."

Amanda chuckled. "You have a point there. A fate worse than any you could find here."

She relived the moments with Lord Saville, and realized

that he had forced a chink in her armor. The world looked as full of promise as the spring day outside. Still she kept this new wonder to herself, afraid that speaking about it would make it disappear.

They stepped downstairs and joined the Dowager in the drawing room. The old lady was sipping brandy, and pressing a handkerchief dampened with eau-de-cologne to her temple. "*That woman* always gives me the worst headache," she began peevishly, but the inevitable harangue was interrupted when Billings knocked and announced a caller, Sir Digby Knottiswood.

The Dowager reacted with scant interest, but ordered the butler to show him into the green salon, the smallest and coziest of the salons, and which the Dowager preferred above all others in the house.

Amanda hastened to greet Sir Digby while Pamela helped the Dowager to straighten her cap and arrange her gray gown in satisfactory folds.

Amanda's thought about her charade with Sir Digby with waning enthusiasm. Her mind was full of the encounter with Lord Saville, but she greeted her supposed beau meekly and offered him a glass of sherry.

The Dowager gave him the full impact of her usual glare, magnified with her quizzing glass. Sir Digby instinctively inserted a pudgy finger between his neck and shirt collar, as if its tight fit were the sole cause of his discomfort.

"Ah, Sir Digby. At last I make your acquaintance. You have been remarkably invisible, even though your roses have filled every vase in this house," the Dowager said with a frown. "A waste of funds, if you ask me. Are you a wastrel, Sir Digby?"

He gulped like a beached fish and Amanda hastened to the rescue. "He's here now, Grandmama." She sat down next to him, giving him an encouraging pat on the arm.

"And not a moment too early." The Dowager archly introduced Lady Pamela, and the two had a blushing contest. Sir Digby's face took on a purplish hue. Their discomfort prodded Amanda into soft laughter. "Pamela, you goose, he won't bite you. In fact, you'd have to search far and wide for a more obliging gentleman."

"Forgive me, but I'm deuced uncomfortable with new acquaintances," Sir Digby confessed reluctantly. "I'm delighted to meet you, Lady Pamela. I have come to invite Miss Bowen for a ride in the park tomorrow, and now I'd like to extend the invitation to you as well."

Pamela brightened at the prospect, but the Dowager put a damper on her enthusiasm.

"She ain't out yet, so you'll have to wait, Sir Digby. But since you're growing closer to Amanda, I'm sure there will be other opportunities to take Lady Pamela for a drive," she added more kindly. "I hope you'll stay for tea."

A glimmer of interest darted into Sir Digby's troubled eyes. "Well—if you insist."

"Of course, I—we'd love to have you," Amanda coaxed, her face wreathed in smiles. Startled, he looked at her exaggerated display of white teeth, then understood her game, and awkwardly squeezed her hand on the sofa.

"Oh, yes, Great-aunt Ambrosia serves a most delicious tea," Pamela chimed in. "You'll love the crumpets and the feather-light sponge cake, and I could—er—*swear* the clotted cream is directly imported from Devon."

"Mind your language. You speak like a Billingsgate fishwife, Pamela," the Dowager snapped, although she was clearly pleased by the flattery. "I think Cook has made some of her cream-filled pastries this afternoon, her specialty."

Amanda read Sir Digby's face, and saw that he had, once crumpets were mentioned, definitely decided to stay for tea. They could all use the invigorating brew after a trying morning, Amanda thought, especially the Dowager, who looked tired after her battle with Lurlene.

Lurlene had been victorious in the end; the ball decor would be left entirely in her hands, and Amanda shuddered at the thought of the splendid Berkley Square ballroom defaced by hundreds of yards of gaudy silk, which was Lurlene's idea of sophistication. Every room Lurlene had ever decorated was smothered in a jarring tone of purplish-pink.

Even the tiny green salon in South Street would be better for the ball than any room decorated by Lurlene's hand, Amanda thought. The green salon at least gave a friendly impression. The walls were covered with forest-green brocade and gilt moldings, and above the fireplace hung an enormous portrait of Amanda's grandfather in full military regalia. The sofas were plump and comfortable and strewn with shawls, magazines, books, embroidery baskets, and watercolor pads indicating the occupant's main interests.

As if the Dowager could read the direction of Amanda's thoughts, she said, "I feel as if I'm returning from a war—and the sad loser. The problem of the ballroom could have been solved more easily had I but ordered Lurlene to wait upon us here. That would have saved us the discomfort of meeting her court of drooling dandies, ready to ogle every person in a petticoat."

Sir Digby blanched at her words, and his disconcerted expression was not lost on the Dowager. "What business your harebrain of a nephew has at Lurlene's door, I don't know," she said to him. "He came into the salon at Berkley Square, calm as you please, without as much as an excuse on his lips. Shocking conduct!"

Sir Digby collected himself, three chins wobbling aggressively. "I believe Saville's manner's something I can't change, however much I've tried. My nephew is a severe trial to his family, but he has always gone his own way. But I suppose one can forgive a man a few flaws." He clasped his paunch as if seeking support. "You mark my words, Lady Bowen, Saville will be cured of this folly for Lurlene ere long."

The Dowager gave him a shrewd glance from the corner of her eye. "I daresay," she said in the driest of tones. She fidgeted with the twined cord of her fan. "His obsession for Lurlene doesn't stop him from setting the rest of the female society a-flutter." She looked directly at Amanda, who swallowed hard.

"The poor chap cannot help that he was born with a handsome face and an abundance of charm—unlike some of us." Sir Digby mopped his brow. "I don't know why we have to talk about my nephew."

Billings, his face a suitable mask of hauteur, carried in a heavy tea tray, and Sir Digby's interest was immediately transferred to the imminent repast. His ruffled feathers were smoothed like magic.

Lady Pamela, who had held herself in the background during the speech, shared Sir Digby's avid interest in food. As she offered to do the honors, they were soon happily chatting about the finer points of cream cakes and custard-filled éclairs. It was hard to judge who was the most knowledgeable on the subject, as Sir Digby and Pamela argued the relative merits of vanilla versus apricot custard. Pamela almost forgot to hand the cups out as the argument heated up. Amanda set a cup and a plate with buttered toast in front of the Dowager and helped herself to an éclair. The tea was sweet and hot on her tongue, making her feel better instantly.

The Dowager rolled her eyes heavenward, silently nibbling on a piece of toast, while Amanda listened to the connoisseurs in amazement. Lady Pamela's face had taken on a glow of happiness as she insisted that a pinch of finely ground cinnamon enhanced the flavor of vanilla, something that Sir Digby opposed with vehemence.

"Digby won't do, you know—for all his eligibility," the Dowager said to Amanda in an undervoice. "You'd be bored to flinders after a week under his roof."

"The prospect cannot be that bad. You said yourself I have to find a husband, and Sir Digby is a very kind-hearted gentleman. He will never browbeat me."

"Perhaps—but he's much too fusty." The Dowager tapped her fingernails on the armrests of her chair. "No, you need a greater challenge, someone with multiple interests, a keen intellect, and stimulating conversation."

When Amanda spoke, her voice was laced with irony. "I suppose you know just the gentleman."

"There must be a full score," the Dowager said airily, without committing herself to names. Taking a sip of tea, she smacked with appreciation. "Tea does a world of good to an old body, and God knows I need it after this latest tribulation with Lurlene. I swear I don't know what Justin sees in her—and to think that a grandchild of mine will have her for a mother." The Dowager raised a gnarled hand to her forehead and closed her eyes with an air of utter resignation.

"I thought you'd be pleased," Amanda said.

The Dowager's hand fell into her lap and she fixed Amanda with an awful eye. "Great-grandchildren are what I want—"

"Pray, don't begin one of your lectures."

"A hearty great-grandson," the Dowager muttered, her eyes suddenly dewy. She snapped her head back. "Tell me, what do you think of Lord Saville?"

Amanda's lips curved smugly and she wiggled a finger under the Dowager's nose. "Grandmama, you cannot pull the wool over my eyes. If you plan to give Lurlene a setdown by using me to divert Saville's ardor, you have windmills in your head."

The Dowager looked very much like a crafty old crow as she cocked her head to the side. "I thought you enjoyed his company this afternoon."

"Fudge! He merely likes the sound of his own voice," Amanda said, her gaze darting about the room. She hoped her grandmother could not read her inner confusion.

"Must have had interesting things to say then, if your high color was any proof," the Dowager commented shrewdly, and left the subject. She involved Sir Digby in a lengthy discussion about the war with France.

Amanda stewed in silence, frightened to examine her feelings for Lord Saville too closely. She knew she ought to loathe the marquess with all her heart, but instead her heart overflowed with enchantment. Knowing him for a ruthless heart-crusher, she had forced herself to avoid him during the previous seasons in London. Now it seemed she had become entangled against her wishes. His charm was spinning an invisible web around her, pulling her firmly toward an abyss of misery.

She wanted to groan with frustration, and vowed to stay away from him at all costs. Mentally listing all the eligible gentlemen of her acquaintance, she dismissed them one by one. And she refused to marry without love. If her foolish heart had decided to fall for Lord Saville, she was headed for disaster, for with him, there was no hope of happiness.

However, *without* him . . . what would her life be worth?

CHAPTER 8

LADY PAMELA'S COME-OUT BALL was destined to be one of the season's gilded events. The shy guest of honor was dressed in a plain white muslin gown of straight empire lines with small puffed sleeves, which flattered her plump figure. Amanda had never seen her friend look so pretty and so happy. Pamela's throat and ears were adorned with pearls, and in her hand dangled a net reticule, its bottom displaying a huge tassel.

Amanda was pleased with her own appearance in her gown of sea-green silk with a scalloped hem that swayed gently as she moved. A lacy white shawl covered her almost bare shoulders, and her raven curls gleamed from the vigorous brushing administered earlier by Meg. Around her neck glittered a thin necklace of diamonds, a birthday gift from the Dowager, and on her wrist, a matching bracelet made its bid for attention.

Amanda saw Lurlene's gaze repeatedly dart toward the Dowager to gauge her reaction to the decor of the ballroom. White funereal lilies sent out a devastating scent, and an enormous purplish-pink silk canopy swathed the entire room, suspended from the arms of hideous cupids in the ceiling. All the pink had a suffocating effect. Curling silver ribbons floated in masses from the silk to the floor to trip up unwary guests. Amanda knew well the Dowager's low opinion of the color scheme, and soon so did others, as the old woman never hesitated to air her views in a loud and penetrating voice.

"I declare, just like one of Gunters' pink ices! I should have known that Lurlene would do something like this just to disgust me."

Amanda silently agreed with the Dowager, since this particular shade of sickly pink wasn't her favorite color. Nevertheless, it was Pamela's ball and she had exclaimed with pleasure at the decorations.

But however stifling the color scheme, the ball was an obvious success from the start. The main reason could be traced to an artificial fountain spouting endless rivers of champagne through golden lions' open maws. "That champagne will be my financial ruin," the Dowager muttered to Amanda.

"Pish," came Amanda's prompt response as she viewed the vast arrangement of pink carnations around the base of the fountain.

"This is like a magical grotto," Pamela commented, stunned by every lavish detail. "Thank you so much, Great-aunt Ambrosia. I know I can never thank you enough."

"Peagoose. Just set about securing a husband. That's what all this is for."

Amanda winked mischievously at her friend. Pamela emanated fascination as she clasped her hands and sighed. Her enormous awestruck eyes and glowing brown hair, which recently had been cut and fashioned *à la Tite*, lent a lightness to her face. She had grown a trifle plumper, but it suited her well.

After leaving Pamela in Lady and Lord Bowen's care by the door, where she was to be presented to the guests as they arrived, Amanda accompanied the Dowager to the row of chairs set up for the chaperones. "Pam won't have any difficulty finding a husband, Grandmama," Amanda said firmly.

The Dowager sank onto one of the very uncomfortable chairs that she scathingly called the "row of old prunes." "Let's hope you're right." The old lady looked regal in her finest Robe à l'Anglaise of dark blue taffeta that billowed around her in a hooped style fashionable forty years earlier. When Amanda had urged her to buy a new fashionable gown for Pamela's ball, she had responded that she didn't hold with "spending the blunt on an old scarecrow" like herself when there were more important matters that needed her support. In her turban bobbed three bushy ostrich feathers, attached to the folds by a huge cameo. Around her neck glittered a garish diamond necklace, and her fingers were ablaze with diamonds, sapphires, and rubies mixed in abandon. The *beau monde* thought the Dowager an eccentric, and looking at her tonight, Amanda tended to agree.

Gentlemen, after meeting Pamela and paying their homage to Lurlene at the door, advanced in an irregular flow to place their names on Amanda's dance card. Most of them were old friends from previous seasons.

"They ain't exactly fighting over you," the Dowager commented sourly. "It was different in my salad days; I had half of the eligible beaus dangling after me. Too bad pink and white complexions are all the rage these days." She scrutinized Amanda's alabaster-tinted cheeks. "If I had deigned to marry that milksop Lord Henley, you'd be blond, I wager—"

"With rabbit teeth and a squint."

The Dowager chuckled. "If your great-grandfather hadn't married that Spanish woman—"

"Ifs—ifs! It doesn't change the fact that I look like a gypsy." An impish smile lifted the corners of Amanda's lips as her gaze rested on Lurlene. "You know, I'd be bored having that gaggle of macaronis and moonlings dogging my footsteps. I don't envy Lurlene in the least. Well, perhaps a trifle, but nothing that signifies."

The Dowager patted Amanda's knee affectionately. "You have superior sense, my gel, and some day—soon I hope—some man other than Sir Digby will wake up and notice your sterling qualities."

Amanda laughed. "I imagine you cannot see any flaw in your offspring."

"Hah! That son of mine has no more sense than Lurlene—and I assure you, that flaw doesn't spring from my side of the family."

The endless arrival of guests, whose attire rivaled the dazzling plumage of peacocks, was rapidly turning the event into a shocking squeeze, a necessary detail for success. The sound of neighing laughs and affected voices rose steadily toward the pink canopy above their heads, and Amanda smiled until she thought her lips would freeze in an up-turned crescent.

After greeting everyone, Lady Pamela looked undeniably dazed as she returned to the ballroom. In agitated tones she sibilated to Amanda, "If you only knew how many damp—and limp—hands I have clasped! I hope I never have to repeat this ordeal."

Amanda laughed. "I know. Well, it's over now and you may dance the night away. This being your debut, you're bound to have admirers aplenty."

Lady Pamela said with grim wisdom, "Don't count on it.

With all those delicious ices at Gunters' and all the sinful cakes at tea, my waist hasn't stopped growing since I came to town. It's daunting to say the least."

"I'm sure most of the gentlemen like a girl with a bit of substance."

Pamela gave a mirthless laugh. "Only men like Sir Digby. Look, there he is—with Lord Saville. I swear they are the last to arrive."

Amanda's heart lurched suddenly as Lord Saville stepped across the threshold. "Always fashionably late. Before now, they paid only perfunctory attendance at balls and routs, and if it weren't for Sir Digby's reason for courting me, they wouldn't be here at all."

Pamela suddenly looked crestfallen, and Amanda regretted her words.

Lord Saville admired Lurlene's splendid emeralds, his hand on her shoulder as she clung to his arm. Had Lord Bowen noticed his shameless maneuver? Amanda's worried gaze found her father across the floor, involved in an amiable discussion with an old friend, the ancient Admiral Riverwood, one of the Dowager's old beaus. Her father didn't keep Lurlene under jealous vigilance, and guffawed at some joke, oblivious to Lord Saville's presence.

"Sir Digby is so very civil toward me, and he has such interesting topics of conversation." Lady Pamela interrupted Amanda's thoughts and squirmed with excitement as he ambled in their direction.

"I daresay," Amanda said dryly, but she looked at her friend with some surprise.

Sir Digby reached the "row of prunes" and bowed handsomely, instantly drawing out one of his ubiquitous handkerchiefs to mop his brow.

"Dear ladies," he wheezed, "delighted to see you."

Amanda thought his gaze lingered a trifle longer than necessary on Lady Pamela's sweet face.

"A dreadful crush, ain't it?" he said after the Dowager's frank nod had given him permission to continue. He addressed the blushing Lady Pamela. "Everyone of any consequence has turned up at your do."

"They wouldn't dare stay away," the Dowager said archly.

The small string orchestra behind a screen of potted palms struck up a tune. Lord Bowen hastened across the room and asked to lead Lady Pamela into the first set. She blushed with pleasure, and stepped with him to the dance floor.

Sir Digby collapsed on her vacated chair, which groaned alarmingly under his weight. "I broke my promise to you, Miss Amanda. I couldn't stop Saville from attending the ball. He said he had some business to take care of, but I can't for the world divine what transactions he might have here." He scratched his triple chin in consternation and shook his head. He was blind to the grim tilt of Amanda's lips as he turned his attention back to her. His face had fallen into folds of misery. "Exhausting activity to keep up this charade of courtship, Miss Bowen," he said in a glum undertone, and leaned an inch closer.

"Very decent of you to attend this event, Sir Digby." She inclined her head sideways and murmured, "Could you manage to look besotted for a moment, just to give the tattlemongers some fuel for their gossip?"

His face changed from misery to dismay as he valiantly struggled to comply. Taking a deep rasping breath he mustered a faltering smile, and Amanda had an irresistible urge to giggle.

"Magnificent," she breathed, and dazzled him with a

wide grin, hoping that at least a couple of guests had noticed their fond exchange.

"I feel like bolting to the country if only to escape this," he stated in injured tones. "Miss Amanda, you're a most unusual female—er—lady." He twisted and turned, the chair protesting loudly.

Amanda smoothed the soft fabric of her gown. "And you don't approve of it?" As he forbore to answer, his eyebrows pleated with misgiving, she cajoled, "But I haven't done anything outside the acceptable. Only you know about our pact."

"Ahem—but don't you see—they all *expect* us to marry now," he complained, his voice thick with discomfort. "It's becoming real."

"You're afraid I will make you go through with it, Sir Digby." She patted his arm with her fan. "I assure you, have no fears on that score. When the season is over, you won't have to see me again."

He sighed with deep relief, and Amanda couldn't repress a chuckle.

"I don't dislike your company," he hurriedly professed. "It's only that I ain't used to this sort of thing."

"I suppose we don't have many interests in common, but perhaps you and Lady Pamela share many views," she said.

Sir Digby whipped his head around to give her a sharp glance, much struck by her words. Amanda nodded in confirmation. A calculating and somewhat eager look crept into his face. Amanda was gratified that she had guessed right. Lady Pamela had captured his interest. Not that he would ever admit such a thing—not yet anyway, she mused, but she would see to it that he spent plenty of time in her friend's company.

Sir Digby puffed and heaved himself to his feet. "I suppose this interlude will suffice to set the tongues wagging." With an air of disgust, he went on, "Now I have to go and do the pretty to our hostess, before I can make my escape."

As he plodded off, Amanda watched the dancing couples. The third set was well under way. Pamela was dancing with Sir Anthony Fanshawe, and Lord Bowen with a neighbor up from the country for the occasion. Lord Saville was standing by the ballroom doors with Lurlene, who glowed with health and beauty. Matching the decor, she wore a dusky pink gown spangled with sequins, whose brilliance competed with the diamonds of her tiara and necklace. Lurlene was very proud of her costly jewels, wedding gifts from her adoring husband. Yes, Lurlene was in fine fettle indeed.

Lord Saville whispered something in Lurlene's ear, and she simpered, squeezing his arm. A wave of anger ripped through Amanda, and she scanned the ballroom for her father who was now talking with a group of men clustered around the champagne fountain. She had to admire him for his innocent trust.

The Dowager kept up a monotonous conversation with an old crony, and Amanda found herself momentarily abandoned. She decided to freshen up, and after murmuring her intentions in the Dowager's ear, she wound her way around the throng of guests toward the door. The music paused, and to her chagrin she saw she was just in time to view the backs of Lord Saville and Lurlene as they climbed the stairs to the second floor where one of the guest rooms was set aside for the ladies' convenience.

Pinching her lips into a thin determined line, Amanda began to ascend the stairs, praying they would not notice her and think she was deliberately spying. Time and time again she had to remind herself that their doings were no concern of hers, but in her chest a stubborn flame of compassion burned for her father. Why had he fallen for Lurlene's superficial charms? Why did she have to be so fickle?

From the corner of her eye she saw them enter Lurlene's private sitting room and she rushed past, hiding her face behind her fan.

The room was well-equipped for the lady guests' needs, and Amanda was relieved to find the chamber empty. She felt no desire to chatter when her thoughts swirled in wild turmoil. First the splashed water on her burning cheeks, then icy eau-de-cologne, to calm herself. The nerve of *that woman*! Amanda fumed and patted some rice powder on her nose and forehead.

Voices rose and fell nearby, and Amanda grew rigid as she recognized her stepmother's exaggerated tone. The wall was very thin since it had been erected long after the mansion had been built for the purpose of creating an extra room. Lurlene's voice droned on, but Amanda couldn't hear her words. Because of Lord Saville's deeper tone, his words were clearly audible.

"Dear Lurlene, you know I never go back on my word, and you shall have your necklace. I did promise you one once." He paused and silence fell, during which Amanda's fertile imagination pictured Lurlene in his arms. He continued, his voice a notch louder, "You deceived me, turned away from me most rudely. But I hold no grudge. I will win you yet, Lurlene. And the necklace, composed of the most superb diamonds and sapphires you'll ever see, is but the first step in a long row of gifts to celebrate your beauty."

"Disgusting!" Amanda grated between clenched teeth, dizzy with rage.

Lurlene cooed with delight, and Amanda pictured her face veiled in sugary smiles. She could have strangled them both at that moment, and her fingers clamped around the rounded edge of the washbasin. She wanted to flee from the room, but her feet had stubbornly grown roots.

"Oh, Keith—you know that I've always held you in high esteem, it's just that—"

"Say no more! It hurts to watch you with Bowen, and I don't know why you chose him before me. The pain of your rejection is unbearable."

Amanda couldn't believe her ears. Never had she pictured Lord Saville as the tragic type, and something in his words didn't ring quite true. Anyway, it was outside of enough that he was closeted in private with Lurlene, promising her costly gifts. What if Father found them there? His anger wasn't easy to provoke, but when his wrath was aroused, he was dangerous. Amanda furrowed her brow. Should she inform him? No, she couldn't bear to be the one to tell him. But the situation couldn't go much further without her father finding out.

After adjusting her short curls, Amanda forced herself toward the door, loath to eavesdrop further but reluctant to chance encountering them.

As soon as she entered the corridor, the door to the sitting room opened, and she had a clear view of Lord Saville standing with his back against the lace-swathed windows. Lurlene emerged from the chamber, her face a deep rose, her eyes sparkling with delight.

"Why, Amanda!" she exclaimed, not in the least embarrassed. "You know, Keith has just promised to present me a handsome necklace. Isn't it extraordinary? I can't wait to see—and wear it!"

Amanda gasped with surprise, and her gaze darted from Lurlene's face to Lord Saville's. An enigmatic smile creased his lean features, and Amanda looked at him in suspicion. Would the gift become public knowledge—a scandal? Lurlene wasn't known to keep secrets for long, and

Amanda trembled at the thought of the pain this incident would cause her father. "I see!" she said in arctic tones. "I'm surprised you approve of gifts from any gentleman but Father."

"Don't be such a starchy goose, Mandy. The necklace is an ode to my bea—to me," Lurlene said with a purr, belatedly conscious of her vanity. "You're envious," she added and flounced down the stairs to boast that she still possessed Lord Saville's devotion.

Vexed, Amanda was about to follow her, and warn her to keep silent, when Lord Saville called, "Amanda." He had stepped to the door and was nonchalantly leaning against the door jamb. His gaze burned darkly into her. He pushed an unruly curl from his forehead and Amanda pictured Lurlene's coy hand ruffling his crisp hair. The image formed a clot of misery in her chest. She could clearly remember the texture of his hair and the steely feel of his biceps. A fire or resentment mixed with longing smoldered in her stomach.

"I suppose you'll rush to your father full of the news," he taunted, his tone bored.

Amanda compressed her lips, not deigning to answer at first, her eyes burning with unshed tears.

"Lord Saville, I don't know what your game is, but for your information, I don't approve of such goings-on."

"You might as well come right out and confess that you were eavesdropping," he goaded, and moved toward her. "Really, my romance with Lurlene isn't the end of the world." His narrowed eyes glinted down at her, and he daringly traced a finger along her jaw, but she slewed her head away from his touch.

"You would say that of course—not caring over whose feelings you ride roughshod. How can you be so nonchalant? You have no heart, milord—always putting yourself first." Amanda's voice cracked, and she was mortified at her display of emotion. His image wavered in front of her as tears clouded her vision, but she refused to brush them away, not for one moment wanting to acknowledge her weakness. She bravely tilted up her chin. "How can you face me so calmly after what you said to Lurlene? I know you're planning to break my father's heart."

"Egad! Looks like yours is broken. Who is the culprit?" he asked softly, his eyes almost tender. "Here, use my handkerchief." He held the white muslin square to her eyes.

Amanda gave his hand a mighty shove away from her face. "Don't touch me!"

Taking a deep breath, he continued, "Your father has more sense than you give him credit for. He deals perfectly with Lurlene, and I assure you, his heart will be intact. He's not jealous of her admirers."

"And you take full advantage of the fact—seizing every opportunity to worm your way into her affection."

"Come now, Miss Bowen. I don't believe for one moment that you care where I bestow my affection." His goading voice sent more anger through her veins. "Do you?"

How neatly he turned situations to his own advantage. "Don't change the subject!" she demanded, but could say no more, as a party of young ladies came running up the stairs toward the guest room, talking excitedly.

A smile lit Lord Saville's eyes, and Amanda drew a shivering breath, plying her fan distractedly.

"This is not the time and place to discuss such an intimate subject as my love life, Miss Amanda. I don't suppose you care to show me the family portraits, if only to give the traces of your distress time to disappear?"

"How could I refuse when you put it like that? But don't think for one moment that you can make an ally out of me.

I abhor your dalliance with my stepmother." She made sure that several feet separated them as she led the way toward the long gallery around the corner. She wished herself elsewhere, but all the while keenly aware of his virile proximity.

He lifted his quizzing glass and stared at the long row of portraits. "Ah! A dour-faced and intimidating lot. I squirm under so many black looks," Saville said with a show of fear as they faced the Bowen ancestors.

Amanda thawed a little, but she knew that had been his aim—to win her over with charm.

He pointed at a haughty gentleman, clad in pleated ruff and trunk hose, frowning down his beaky nose at the viewer. "He looks remarkably like your grandmother, Miss Bowen. Can you be sure she wasn't the model for this portrait?"

Amanda couldn't stop a laugh at the thought of the Dowager's thin legs encased in trunk hose and her feet in shoes with upturned toes.

"How excessively naughty of you to suggest such a thing. Anyone can see that this portrait was painted a long time ago. It has been restored several times."

He laughed, a low roguish sound. "Your grandmother's stern face could curl the paint on any picture."

Amanda squared her shoulders in defiance. "You clearly don't hold my family in high esteem. First you court my father's wife, then you insult my grandmother, and treat me without the least consideration."

He took a step closer, a wicked light shining in his deepset eyes. "You're by far the most interesting of the lot."

Amanda sucked in her breath with outrage. "Don't waste your compliments on me, milord. I'm not so easily taken in—not like Lurlene, you know. Nothing you say can make me switch sides and sanction your courtship of my foolish stepmother."

"You're a sharp one, Miss Bowen, and very hard on a poor chap, always taking me to task for sincerely offered compliments. You have to learn to accept—"

"Desist, do!" Amanda swung away and turned her back to him, her face stormy.

He sighed audibly. "I know when I'm beaten." He returned his attention to the portraits. "All my forefathers seem to resemble either Digby or my hatchet-faced sister, Agatha. Mine is not a family of much distinction, I'm afraid."

Amanda crossed her arms over her chest. "I suppose *your* features would enliven the Saville row of portraits," she said sarcastically, still facing away.

"I wasn't fishing for a compliment. Besides, an infirm leg—" He bent to rub his leg absentmindedly.

Amanda gave a small snort. "Such a minor flaw wouldn't show on the picture, surely." Thinking for a moment, she shot him a dark sideways glance. "Tell me, does it bother you not to be—perfect?"

He laughed, a dry flat sound. "How glum we are! You want to know if I am bitter about my injury. That's a rather personal question, don't you think? Some might say you were prying into my murky secrets."

Amanda hesitated, studying him cautiously. "We have never minced words before, so why start now?"

He shifted the cane to his other hand. "*That's* what I like about you, Miss Bowen, your frank approach. Well, then I'm honor-bound to inform you that this flaw," he flippantly pointed at his leg, "does anger me sometimes, especially in wet weather when it aches abominably. Then I become like a bear with a sore head." He bent a thoughtful gaze on his cane, his air suddenly serious. "Well—plainly speaking—I try to ignore the pain, because I'll have to live with it for the rest of my life—the broken bone didn't set right, y'see." He reached out and slid the pad of his right forefinger along her chin, whipping up a whirlwind of confusing emotions within her. "As for vanity, I dare hope I'm no worse than the rest of the fops here tonight," he added wryly.

"Please," she whispered, unable to tear herself away from his magic touch, "stop pursuing my stepmother. You will only cause harm."

"She must have made your life difficult. You had your father all to yourself and then Lurlene came and took him away from you, actually pushing you out of your comfortable nest."

His words touched the sore spot in her heart that she so valiantly had struggled to overcome since her father's and Lurlene's wedding. "I admit it was difficult, but I don't believe I have the right to judge my father's actions. Besides, I'm grown, and not expected to live with him for the rest of my life."

"Of course. You're supposed to get married and start your own family." His voice lowered suggestively. "With Sir Digby perhaps?"

"You have no right—"

"You *are* an attractive little confection. Would you like to have Lurlene's place in my heart?" he murmured, his breath tickling her face.

Outraged, Amanda wrenched herself free. "Of course not! You must be dimwitted to believe that I'd accept your insincere compliments and fall into your arms."

"I had no such plans," he said dryly, his shoulders lifting in a sigh. "You're charming, that's all. Besides, I had almost forgotten Digby's claim on you. He'll call me out if he finds me here."

Amanda still fought the excitement his touch had stirred

up within her. "I thought you had no scruples about courting other gentlemen's wives or fiancées," came her severe rejoinder.

Cynicism lay like a cold mask on his features. "Adds spice to the adventure, don't you think?"

Amanda's eyes flashed fire. "Obviously your conscience doesn't assail you overly much."

"Not unduly." He put his hand on her shoulder, pulling her hard toward him as he gazed down at her flushed face. "How righteous you are! Little Saint Amanda," he teased, cupping her neck with one strong hand. She tried to drag herself away, a useless endeavor, as the shock of his hard body against hers paralyzed any action. He smelled wonderfully of shaving soap and crisp linen, plus that elusive male scent that made her senses swim.

Her breathing coming in small gasps, she stared fixedly as his sensuous lips closed the distance between them. Shutting her eyes, she received the demanding pressure of his mouth on hers. Joy, rage, and humiliation fought within her, while her conscience chided her for surrendering.

His arm crushed her even closer to him, his lips moving hungrily over hers, and her head reeled with the potent power of his seduction, and his claret-flavored kiss. Her fingers sought the springy curls at the nape of his neck, reveling in the sensation. The allure of his broad shoulders under her arms, the scent, the strength of him, knocked her senseless just like it had on the night of their first kiss. He stoked a raging fire in her blood, and she clung closer to seek its quenching.

With a jerk he pulled himself away. "Darling," he murmured huskily. "You're supposed to shun my advances."

Amanda couldn't answer as a tremor shuddered through her in the aftermath of his heart-robbing assault. Wishing he were any gentleman but Lord Saville, she kept her eyes tightly closed, her cheek pressed into his chest.

"Who could have suspected such ardor under that cool exterior," he said, his voice laced with amazement. "I'm quite bowled over."

"Oh, cease this instant! Your kisses are nothing but part of your infernal campaign against my family—and I'm behaving idiotically," she said with a sob, and tore herself away from his spell. "I'm convinced you're going to brag wide and long about my wanton behavior."

His fierce grip on her shoulder stunned her into silence. "Listen. I didn't plan on this happening, Amanda. I've never looked upon you with amorous intent. And my dealings with Lurlene have nothing to do with you, I swear it."

"Don't they?" Amanda breathed, her eyes widening in pain. "What affects my family, affects me."

"Oh, blast it all! Forget what I just said," he ordered in chilly tones. Straightening, he took a deep breath. She sensed that he was pulling away from her and from his own emotions. His expression was flat and cold as he continued, "I'm behaving like a dead bore. Forgive me if you can, Amanda." A hint of sorrow crept into his eyes. "I assure you, I don't seek to deliberately hurt you."

Amanda contemplated his words in stark silence as she watched him walk away, his uneven steps ringing on the gleaming parquet and echoing in her head. Had she read guilt in his eyes?

CHAPTER 9

THE NIGHT WAS OLD when the marquess returned to the Saville mansion on Grosvenor Square. After the ball, he had joined a cardgame at Brooks's and came home considerably plumper in the pocket, a windfall which failed to cheer him. He dreaded the moment when he had to be alone with his disturbing thoughts. Nevertheless, the time arrived when he stepped into his dark study for a glass of brandy before retiring. At once the thoughts crowded in like malevolent ghosts.

He sat down in a wingchair and massaged his leg which nagged him with a dull throbbing ache. Gloomily studying the dark-green velvet curtains by the majestic windows, and his vast collection of books in the cherrywood bookcases, Keith pondered the events of the evening. Everything was going as planned; Lurlene had taken the bait like a greedy fish, and now time, and the gossips, would do the rest. But instead of feeling triumphant, a restlessness ate him, a doubt chewed on his mind that he was doing the wrong thing. The sole cause for his doubt was Amanda Bowen.

His lips tightened. What did Amanda Bowen's attitudes

matter to him? She was just another hysterical female, arguing and crying. But however much he wanted to deny it, Amanda had kindled passion and a bittersweet ache in his heart. He actually *liked* her. She wasn't beautiful in the fragile way of a hothouse flower like Lurlene, but she had charm and intelligence beneath that stern little face. And from what he had discovered, her slender body was capable of fierce passion.

He sighed and, inexplicably depressed, took a deep draught of brandy. If Dig could win Amanda's hand, then Dig would be a very lucky man indeed, he thought, staring unseeing at the beige and burgundy Oriental carpet. The last thing he wanted to do was to ruin old Dig's chances for happiness.

Keith slammed the snifter into the empty grate, the crash shattering the stillness. Why did he suddenly resent old Dig's chances at happiness with Amanda?

In South Street, not many blocks from the Saville mansion, Amanda and Lady Pamela were lying on top of Amanda's bed, chatting about the ball. Wrapped in dressing gowns generously trimmed with French lace, they sipped hot cocoa. The room was heated by a fire in the grate, and the light from the flames leaped and danced on the light-blue wallpaper patterned with white flowers. The bed hangings, edged with gold tassels, carried the same pattern as the walls, and the velvet curtains by the two narrow windows were blue.

Lady Pamela's eyes shone like bright stars. "I have never had a more exhilarating evening," she admitted with a deep sigh of pleasure. "Can you imagine—all of it for me."

"Yes, and you were an instant success. The gentlemen literally fell over each other to secure a dance with you. I'm so pleased," Amanda said, although her thoughts were not quite on the topic of Pamela's ball.

"And I danced every dance," Pamela went on. "Everybody was so polite."

"And well they should be—with champagne flowing and a succulent supper of lobster patties, truffles, and patés," Amanda pointed out. "Furthermore, no one would dare to snub you in Grandmama's presence. Mark my words, this ball will be talked about as one of the most splendid dos of the season, although I didn't care for the decor."

Pamela's face took on a dreamy quality and she tugged at a wayward curl. "I don't know. I quite like pink silk. It's so—well, romantic."

Amanda refrained from arguing the point. "Did you meet any gentlemen to your liking?"

"You sound just like Great-aunt Ambrosia. Imagine her glaring at me through her eyeglass and booming, 'Weeell, when are you getting married, Peagoose?' " Pamela giggled and squirmed on the blue down quilt, folding her legs under her. "I can't say I've met anyone nicer than Sir Digby, but from what I understand, he's courting you."

Amanda traced the pattern of the quilt with one slender finger, and peered cautiously at the younger woman.

Lady Pamela's cheeks grew rosy, and a shadow of guilt invaded her eyes. "Don't worry, Amanda, I have no designs on him—but I cannot lie about the fact that I find him a most interesting person. I never tire of his company."

"Oh," was all Amanda could say, debating silently whether she should divulge the secret about her pact with Sir Digby. "You don't take offense at his—vast person?"

Pamela pursed her lips thoughtfully. "There is something comfortable about such a *large* man, although I readily admit he could slim down a stone or two."

Amanda laughed. "Ladies are not supposed to have an

opinion on the size of *bodies,* you know, especially not gentlemen's bodies. If Great-aunt Elfina heard you talk like this, she would surely give you a beargarden jaw, and bundle you off back to the country."

"Yes, of course. Grandmother would have one of her fits—but not Great-aunt Ambrosia, I wager. She would merely laugh and agree with me."

"Hmmm, I doubt it. Grandmama never censors her words, but that doesn't mean she wants us to behave similarly. I know she doesn't hold with Sir Digby's ample girth." Amanda smiled wryly. "Fortunately she hasn't told *him* that, *yet.* I live in constant fear of that day. You know Grandmama rarely can keep an opinion to herself."

Pressing a hand to her mouth, Lady Pamela stifled a laugh, her hazel eyes gleaming. "I declare you're as bad as she is. Living here with her gives you that cynical outlook on things." She sighed and watched Amanda slowly sip her cocoa. "And you—do you accept Sir Digby's—*flaw*?"

Amanda stared into space and her fingers clenched around the cup. "He is a very decent gentleman, but I don't love him," she said quietly. She sighed. "To tell you the shocking truth, I've made a pact with Sir Digby. He doesn't want to get married, and I don't want to listen to Grandmama's lectures about my unmarried state, so we decided to pretend—"

"Oh, how infamous!" Pamela's eyes were round with amazement. Her rosy cheeks paled and her hand trembled around the cup. "What if Great-aunt Ambrosia finds out?"

Amanda studied her friend's face narrowly. Pamela cared about Sir Digby. A lot. "She won't find out unless you tell her."

"But what about your courtship?" Pamela looked so bereft that Amanda wanted to end her charade with Sir Digby that very moment.

"I've promised to jilt him at the end of the season."

"Oh." Pamela's lips were tight with disappointment. "It means that he never wants to marry—*anyone.*"

Amanda hugged her. "Oh, I'm not so sure about that. I think Sir Digby will come around to the idea of marriage before the season is over. One thing is for sure, I will never wed him. But you might—"

Lady Pamela gasped and clasped a hand to her heart. "Me? No . . . But how can you be so calm about the pact? I'd never dare pull the wool over Great-aunt Ambrosia's eyes. Come to think of it, your scheme is the most harebrained idea I've ever heard of. And the gall of Sir Digby!"

Amanda smiled at the memory of her meeting with him earlier at the ball. "He doesn't enjoy doing the pretty. I believe he's almost *frightened* of me, and all that courtship entails. For instance, he abhors balls. The dinner-table and card room are his sole interest at gatherings. And you have to admit that his figure doesn't cut a dash on the dance floor."

"I heartily agree on that score," Pamela said, laughing. "His corset *creaks* so."

"Pam! Your language." Amanda was relieved to hear Lady Pamela giggle. Somehow she would convince Sir Digby that he was in love with Pamela and that a marriage to her would be the best solution for everyone.

"I must admit that Digby doesn't hold a candle to his nephew, Lord Saville, who is so very attractive—in a dark sort of way. He's positively daunting," Pamela said.

"I know, but Sir Digby is worth a thousand Savilles," Amanda said gloomily.

Pamela studied her with considerable shrewdness. "I'm not so sure of that. Like Great-aunt Ambrosia, Lord Saville hides a vulnerable heart behind a domineering exterior."

Amanda's eyes grew wide. "I've never thought of him like that. He's a blackguard all the way down to the tips of his polished boots," she said, and pinched her lips together.

"Well, I don't know about that. I assure you, if he's anything like Great-aunt Ambrosia, he carefully conceals his true feelings. You know that your old tartar of a grandmother has a heart of gold. Why, just look at the gifts she literally poured over me when I arrived, and now the ball."

"But not without grumbling over it."

"Pshaw! She only likes to appear intimidating so that we won't forget her, or bundle her off to the country to wither away."

Amanda shook her head. "We could never *bundle* Grandmama anywhere and live to tell about it. Pam, you're so kind; you see good in everybody. Don't you understand? Grandmama likes to belittle whatever Great-aunt Elfina has done for you over the years. Believe me, Grandmama makes sure that every little detail of your progress reaches Elfina's long ear."

"Surely Lord Saville isn't scheming like that."

Amanda's eyebrows pulled into an angry frown. "He's worse! I don't know what sort of game he's playing with Lurlene, but it's bound to bring disaster. And my father is a nincompoop for not seeing what's going on right under his nose. Oh, Pamela, what shall I do?" Amanda fished a handkerchief from her pocket and twisted it between her hands. "I feel like warning Father, but I can't help but think the matter's none of my business." She thumped her fist into a pillow.

Lady Pamela looked surprised. "Amanda, it can't be that bad. You must be exaggerating. Why, Lurlene positively *clings* to Lord Bowen—adores him."

Amanda swallowed a sob. She clamped her lips shut so

as not to vent her anger and frustration about Lurlene's behavior at the ball.

Pamela patted her shoulder. "Please don't worry—time will show; and you're right; it's a matter purely between Uncle Justin and Lurlene. However much Lord Saville may resent it, she chose Lord Bowen over him. Lord Saville is a shade too intimidating. When he looks at me, I want to fall through the floor."

"Don't speak that name! I abhor him," Amanda groaned into the pillow. She felt a tightening in her chest and struggled to subdue the emotions that stirred at the mere mention of Lord Saville's name. How could she love a man whom she detested? Miserable, Amanda longed for the old carefree days when she had been untouched by Cupid's cruel arrow. If this *anguish* inside was love, she'd rather live without it.

Two days later, Lord Bowen alighted from his carriage at the Dowager's door in South Street. It was a bright spring day with sunshine smiling equally on the sooty brick facades of the London buildings and the exquisite nodding heads of daffodils and tulips in the park. As she saw him through the window, Amanda ached to speak with him about Lurlene.

She was keeping her grandmother company in the morning room, while Lady Pamela was enjoying a drive in the park with another debutante she had met at the ball. Billings held the door for Lord Bowen, who entered with a cheerful greeting on his lips.

"Papa!" Amanda called joyously, and put aside her embroidery to give him a hug.

"By Jupiter, I couldn't expect a fonder reception had I spent a year in India," he said with a booming laugh. With a flash of concern in his eyes, he looked down at her upturned face and touched one pale cheek. "You look a trifle peaked, my dear Mandy. Are the balls and routs becoming too much for you?"

"Twaddle!" muttered the Dowager, and when Lord Bowen turned to her, she proffered a wrinkled cheek for him to kiss. "Mandy is fit as a fiddle. Due to Lurlene's interesting condition you see female weakness everywhere. I wager she does nothing but fill your ears with tales of misery—and blaming it all on you into the bargain."

Lord Bowen looked uncomfortable under the ruthless onslaught. Sitting down on the hard settee, he smiled sheepishly. "She is so very young, and one has to make concessions—"

"Bah! More fool you, son. She has you exactly where she wants you—around her shrewd little finger." The Dowager glared at him with distaste.

"Surely you're exaggerating, Grandmama," Amanda said in her father's defense. Her eyes, concentrating once more on the embroidery frame, twinkled wickedly, though a wave of pity rippled through her. Gentlemen in love were totally blind. Lord Saville was another example of that.

Lord Bowen sighed, fiddling with the fobs clustered on a gold chain over his yellow-striped waistcoat. "Lurlene's a young innocent, and I cherish the opportunity to take care of her—just like I did Amanda, until she fled the nest." His face had the look of a sad dog, and Amanda's heart constricted at remembering their happy carefree existence before Lurlene's time. "I was lonely for a while, Papa, but I'm used to the change in your marital status now."

The Dowager's snort told its own story, and Amanda noticed from the corner of her eye that her grandmother had sucked in her breath, struggling to control her temper.

"I had hoped you'd reconsider accompanying us to Bowen Court after the season, Mandy," he said. "Lurlene needs company her own age to help her through these trying months."

"But surely not *females*," the Dowager said in disgust, losing her hard-gained control before Amanda had time to speak.

Lord Bowen looked taken aback, and his thick eyebrows pulled into a black bar above his nose. "What do you mean—not females? Surely not children. Lurlene couldn't stand to have boisterous children around her at a time like this," he said, obviously perplexed.

The Dowager's mouth fell open and her eyes almost popped. Amanda heard her murmur, "That blockhead can't be a son of mine."

Amanda jumped into the fray. "Lurlene has seen enough of me this season, chaperoning me everywhere, and I think you should enquire of her whom she wishes to invite. Besides, you knew that I would 'flee the nest' sooner or later, and I'm very content here." Yet, there was the familiar twinge of pain, that feeling of being left out.

The Dowager seldom minced her words, and this was not one of those times. "Son, have you heard the latest gossip about a diamond necklace Saville is planning to bestow on Lurlene—some gift he intended to give her before she became riveted to you?"

Lord Bowen barked a laugh. "Yes, who hasn't? If he wants to throw away his blunt on somebody who won't give anything in return, that's his business."

The Dowager's breath rasped audibly, and Amanda's industrious hands lay still as she stared in wonderment at her father.

He continued, "Yes, it's a boost to Lurlene's flagging spirits knowing that she's desired, and that her beauty is as blinding as it was last year—even though she's increasing. I assure you, her love has never swayed from me."

"But Saville—" The Dowager said with a sputter of outrage.

"I know—he's a very attractive young man, but Lurlene needs an older man to take care of her. She would never deal well with a man like Saville," he said with such conviction that Amanda almost believed him. But a doubt still worried her; had Lurlene managed to pull the wool over his eyes so thoroughly that he couldn't see farther than his own nose? Amanda suspected that only time would tell.

The Dowager voiced her disbelief in acid tones. "I hope you're right, dear Justin. By the way, where is Lurlene *now*?"

"Abed with a bottle of hartshorn clutched in her hand, and the abigail rubbing her feet," he answered without hesitation. Amanda was convinced, although she read skepticism in the Dowager's eyes.

"Very well. The only thing I can say: keep your daylights open, Justin," commanded the Dowager.

He stiffened. "I know that you never approved of my marriage to Lurlene, Mother, but if you're trying to come between us, or to sow suspicion in my mind, I can only beg you to desist. I'm quite capable of managing my own affairs." He sighed. "I came here with the sole purpose of visiting Amanda, and to persuade her to join us at Bowen Court this summer. But it looks like I've come in vain."

Amanda softened immediately. "If it would please you that much, I'll visit you for a few weeks," she promised impulsively, and placed a hand on his arm, while regretting her hasty capitulation.

He looked pathetically pleased, and at that moment Amanda understood that he harbored hidden fears of neglecting his duties toward her. "I love you," she whispered and kissed his cheek. "And I'm truly happy with Grandmama."

Clearing his throat, Lord Bowen rose, handsome and vigorous in the latest fashions. He bowed in front of the Dowager, kissed Amanda on her forehead, then strode out of the room.

"Hrmph!" snorted the Dowager, unusually cowed.

"I declare, Father is the kindest person in the world," Amanda said with daughterly affection. "I do hope for his sake that he's right about Lurlene."

"Flummery!" was the Dowager's opinion, and with an air of total dissatisfaction, she buttoned up her lips.

In the evening, Billings offered a silver salver bearing a missive on heavy cream paper to Amanda. She eyed the folded and sealed message with surprise. After opening it, she scanned the almost illegible scrawl. "It's from Sir Digby," she told the Dowager and Lady Pamela. "He's inviting Pam and me to a picnic at Richmond Park on Wednesday—if this glorious weather holds."

She glanced at Pamela, who was laboring over the next to impossible task of rectifying an error on a watercolor painting. "What do you think? Should we accept? The footman is waiting for an answer."

"Of course, you goose," snapped the Dowager. "You may rest assured that Sir Digby's picnic basket will be full of delicacies, and 'twill do you good to breathe country air for a day."

Lady Pamela gave Amanda a quizzical smile. "It's all very well," she said, "but who is going to be my escort if Sir Digby is yours?"

"You don't need one at the picnic—besides, I'm sure that Sir Digby has made up a party."

Amanda was right on that score, but when she met her fellow guests, she hotly regretted accepting the invitation.

CHAPTER 10

"AT LEAST the sun is shining." Sir Digby squinted toward the cloudless sky as he ponderously heaved himself into the landau that would convey the party to Richmond.

He glowered at his nephew, who already occupied a space on the long seat upholstered with beige velvet. "I will never know how you managed to bully me into this, nevvy," he said with a huff, and collapsed onto the seat.

Keith smiled, unperturbed. "You have to cultivate your acquaintance with Miss Amanda, and since I know how much you dislike to be alone with any female, I offered to accompany you. As simple as that."

"Very well, but why did we have to invite Sir Anthony Fanshawe and Lurlene?" Sir Digby mopped his forehead, where perspiration was gathering rapidly.

"Lurlene will act as chaperone, and Lady Pamela needs an admirer not to feel like the fifth wheel."

Sir Digby cleared his throat. "Not even I, shy that I am, would be a selfish oaf and let a female feel unwelcome, and well you know it, Keith. I don't like your schemes—nothing good ever comes out of them," he said ominously.

"Furthermore, I know this is your excuse to meet Lady Bowen away from Lord Bowen."

"There may be some truth to that."

"Botheration, Keith! How can you be such a cold fish? I'm heartily tired of your rum intrigues."

"I perfectly well know your views on the matter," the marquess said in impassive tones, and yawned behind his gloved hand.

The landau came to a halt at Sir Anthony's lodgings in Half Moon Street. The young man bounded into the carriage. He was a dandy of the first stare, dressed in impeccable dove-gray pantaloons and a dashing waistcoat of yellow-striped satin. Gaping, he stared at Lord Saville's snowy neckcloth, which contrasted sharply with the owner's dark features. Despite the perfect cravat, Lord Saville had loosened his dress code to buckskins and topboots. Sir Anthony absorbed every detail with a small frown, evidently disapproving of such nonchalance.

The next stop was Berkley Square, where Lord Saville alighted to collect Lurlene. Sir Digby's irritation mounted as the horses had to be walked around the square twice, waiting for the tardy lady to emerge from the house. He went so far as to remark to Sir Anthony that the evening would surely be hard upon them before they reached Richmond. But when Lurlene appeared, he hastily swallowed his next biting comment, and stared.

Lurlene certainly looked a vision, that he had to admit. He held out a pudgy hand to assist her into the landau, and Lord Saville climbed in after her, placing his cane on the floor.

"Good-morning," she greeted brightly as she settled her delicate pale pink muslin gown around her. Dainty satin slippers with ribbons criss-crossing the top of her feet were drastically ill-chosen for venturing into the country. However, Lurlene was blissfully unaware of that fact as she smiled seductively at Lord Saville. *The snake! No wonder Keith was so hopelessly besotted.* Sir Digby cursed her silently.

Completely in control, Lurlene twirled her lace-trimmed sunshade and batted her eyelashes.

When the carriage pulled up before the house in South Street, Amanda and Lady Pamela were already waiting in the hallway. Due to his bulk, Sir Digby hesitated to alight, and Lord Saville took the hint and stepped down to escort the ladies to the carriage. His eyebrows rose as the Dowager confronted him in the open door, and the Bowen black look stabbed him through her quizzing glass. Then she studied the rest of the company in the landau, and immediately bristled up. "Don't think for one moment I'll let my lambs go unescorted into this den of foxes," she said to Lord Saville, loud enough for the others—and a passing fishmonger with a wheelbarrow—to hear every word. Her indrawn breath hissed with outrage as her gaze, magnified by the quizzing glass, landed on Lurlene.

"Well! If this doesn't beat it all! Lurlene, I should have guessed it. I'm sorely needed in the capacity of chaperone, that much is clear," she boomed and descended the stairs, her tiny form regal as she elbowed Lord Saville out of the way.

Sir Digby fidgeted, reluctant to share his outing with the old dragon. He was put out that she would dare to press her company upon him without an invitation. However, her presence had to be accepted in grating silence; there was nothing he could do, unless he called off the whole affair.

His countenance brightened somewhat when spying Amanda and Pamela on the stairs. They both looked pretty in light pastel muslin gowns, sensible pelisses and half boots. He thought Lady Pamela looked especially pleasant in a gypsy straw bonnet with blue satin ribbons tied under her chin. He also observed the cold glance Amanda shot his nephew as she refused his aid. With a sheepish face, Keith was left to escort Lady Pamela, who gracefully placed her fingertips on his forearm. There was something so engaging about Lady Pamela, perhaps her unfailingly good humor and modesty, thought Sir Digby. He had momentarily forgotten Amanda, and Sir Anthony hastily assisted her into the landau.

Like the Dowager, Amanda had been taken aback at Lord Saville's presence on their doorstep, and the thought of having to spend even five minutes in his company sent a rivulet of unease along her spine. In an effort to shut him out, she set her parasol at an angle to shield her face from him. But she could do nothing to stop her heart from racing in her chest at the very thought of his presence.

It was a discomfited group that set out toward Richmond, and Sir Digby conjured up visions of his solitary study and favorite chair. He discreetly tried to alleviate the pressure of his neckcloth, which was tied in the Mail Coach style— numerous folds and a large knot—and intensely uncomfortable on his stocky neck.

Lurlene looked with smug satisfaction at the young women on the seat next to her. Deliberately turning her back on the Dowager, she spoke to Amanda. "Why, my dear stepdaughter, you outshine us all today," she said in her sugary voice, and eyed Amanda's simple gown with a smirk. "I could have sworn I've seen that dress several times before. I do hope Mama doesn't scrimp your dress allowance."

Amanda felt an immense reluctance to speak, but she smiled blandly. "Lurlene, you know none of us can hold a candle to your beauty, but I'm very content at the moment," she lied. "And I wouldn't dream of disturbing this jaunt by discussing old gowns, as it's bound to bore the gentlemen to death."

Lurlene pulled back, slightly ruffled. "Of course. We mustn't bore our escorts." She tapped the toe of one slipper peevishly on the floor.

"Don't worry your pretty heads about us," soothed Sir Anthony, beaming pointedly at her. "You look fine as fivepence, Lurlene. We couldn't have wished for lovelier company."

"Perhaps a more *cheerful* one," Lord Saville ventured.

The Dowager gave a disdainful snort, and Amanda's gaze flew to the marquess's face. She saw the usual devil lurking in his smoky eyes.

"It all depends on one's company," came the Dowager's tart rejoinder, but nothing could stir Lord Saville's ire. Sir Digby looked rather put out, thought Amanda, and she bestowed a warm smile on him. "For my part I think Sir Digby is excessively kind to have invited us all. This is a perfect day for a picnic, and I'm looking forward to breathing some fresh air," she said.

"Indeed," chimed Lady Pamela, and as she smiled at Sir Digby, Amanda noticed the slow flush creeping above his collar.

"We must pray that the weather will hold, and that there will be no ants or wasps to ruin the outing," Lurlene interjected with a disapproving catch in her voice. Her nose was tilted at a more upward angle than usual, and the corners of her lovely lips drooped downward, since Lord Saville spent most of his time gazing everywhere but at the occupants of the landau.

"Unfortunately there is nothing we can do about avoiding pesky insects. They don't make an exception for us. We're all victims—no matter how exalted the titles we possess," Sir Digby said with some vinegar in his voice.

The Dowager let out a crow of mirth and earned a withering stare from her daughter-in-law. Sniffing audibly, Lurlene turned to Lord Saville.

"Keith, do something! They are making a mockery of me, when I'm only trying to be polite."

Before Lord Saville could answer, Sir Anthony jumped to the rescue, bravely trying to soothe Lurlene's offended sensibilities. "I'm sure Sir Digby's lackeys have chosen a perfect spot to set up the table, and I promise you won't come to any harm."

"I detest insects almost as much as I detest wearing the same dress twice—or one identical to that of another lady," Lurlene informed them, and Amanda hid a smile behind her fan. "It's the worst *faux pas*," Lurlene continued, giving Amanda's dress a disdainful glance.

"A most interesting point," Lord Saville said dryly. "I do hope you don't feel the same about jewelry, as Lord Bowen would be hard pressed to constantly buy you new stones."

"Ohhh," cooed Lurlene, much mollified, and pounced on the subject that had been simmering in her mind the whole morning. "When are you going to give me the necklace you promised me?"

Amanda was distressed to find that Lord Saville's pledged gift was common knowledge. Evidently Lurlene had bragged about it everywhere, and it was clear that the marquess didn't bother to keep it a secret. Very bad form, Amanda fumed silently, angry with herself for housing warm feelings for such a rake as Lord Saville.

"I will deliver the necklace in three weeks, and I want you to wear it to Almack's. I guarantee it'll outshine all the jewels ever worn in that stuffy place."

The Dowager drew in a long sibilant breath, and thrust her face within two inches of his. "Wretch! I've never met a man of shabbier conduct." Addressing Sir Digby, she ordered, "I want this carriage turned around this instant! I refuse to share a conveyance with a man who deliberately, and openly, tries to ruin my son's marriage. This is a severe trial to my nerves!"

"Don't get into a pelter, Lady Bowen—very bad for your health," drawled Lord Saville. "What would I do with the diamonds? I know of no one who could wear them with such style as Lurlene. The necklace was especially designed for her, long before her marriage to Bowen, and I daresay he hasn't complained about my intention to give it to Lurlene—understanding fellow that he is."

"Your *intention* is very clear. I wager Lurlene will pay heavily for the necklace, and not in money," the Dowager spat, her plumes whipping in every direction. "My son must be excessively thimblewitted to accept such a thing." She sank back onto the seat, gloomy and deflated.

Amanda felt a surge of mortification at having their private business aired abroad, and she hoped that Sir Anthony and Sir Digby wouldn't carry this conversation further. An overpowering urge to smash the mockery from Lord Saville's face came over her, and she gave him a poisonous glare. At least he had some small shred of decency as he bowed to the Dowager and said,

"I'm sorry if I offended you, Lady Bowen, but I assure you—I have no designs to ruin Lord Bowen." He sent Lurlene a calculating glance. "And you have to admit that a beauty like Lurlene's only comes along every hundred years."

Amanda could almost see her stepmother's head growing at those words, and she knew that the outing had been saved, right on the brink of outright disaster. She had to give it to him; Lord Saville was very smooth.

Lurlene simpered, but Sir Digby did somewhat put a

damper on her glory by pointing out that Olivia Lexington's beauty wasn't far below that of Lurlene.

The Dowager cut in, "Addle-brained, that's what you are, Saville, if you're willing to part with your blunt in such a fashion. You could always sell the diamonds—or give them to your long-suffering sister in France."

"But you see, the necklace was specially designed for Lurlene—with sapphires the exact color of her eyes."

"Ohhh, *sapphires*! Keith, I can't wait to see the sapphires. They are my favorite stones," Lurlene said breathlessly, completely restored to happiness at being the center of attention once more.

With slitted eyes Amanda scrutinized Lord Saville's face. Saville was too smooth, too unperturbed, and too— cold. That was it! Where did his coldness stem from? Amanda sensed that his dalliance with Lurlene had a deeper layer that she could not begin to uncover. While her brain eagerly searched for the answer to his strange interest in her stepmother, Amanda's heart contracted with longing and pain. At all cost she had to squelch her attraction for him.

To Lurlene's obvious chagrin, the subject of the necklace was dropped as the landau reached the park at Richmond and the warm, clean air filled their lungs. Tempers that had been frayed were now mellowed, and the sight of Sir Digby's lackeys setting up a large table in the shade of a huge elm, and spreading a starched damask table cloth, filled everyone with expectation. Sir Digby's culinary delights were a byword in the *beau monde*, and an invitation to one of his feasts much coveted.

Amanda breathed deeply of the golden air, the scent of flowering jasmine riding sweetly on the wind. The sun caressed her upturned face, and the grass was a soft yielding carpet under her feet, so different from the relentless stone pavement in the city.

"Shall we take a walk?" queried Sir Digby, holding out his arm to her. He peered with misgiving at the narrow sand path riddled with potholes. Due to his paunch, he had long since forgotten the shape of his feet, and a walk anywhere but along the familiar floor of his lodgings was hazardous at best.

Amanda smiled kindly, her eyes gleaming with mischief. "Don't you have to keep an eye on your staff?"

"I should hope not! They have been thoroughly trained, and my valet knows my taste to the minutest of details," he said, somewhat piqued.

"I beg your pardon, Sir Digby."

"I thought this would be our only chance to keep up our charade," he wheezed. "Later on I'll have to play the host to my ill-assorted guests. If you'll pardon me, dear Miss Amanda, I find it very tiresome to keep the old Lady Bowen content. She has clearly taken me in violent dislike, as well as my nephew."

Amanda let out a laugh. "Yes, she is a handful, I grant you that, but don't fancy that she has singled you out—her discontent encompasses the whole world. Truly, I tried to dissuade Grandmama from joining us, and she almost consented, but my effort came to naught when she clapped eyes on Lord Saville and Lurlene." In an apologetic tone, she added, "She seems to think that she has to keep an eye on them for my father's sake."

Sir Digby heaved a massive sigh. "I don't blame her. My nephew is running a rum sort of game, but I cannot begin to unravel his motives. And you must know that I heartily disagree with him on most points, although I'm deuced fond of the cawker. Mark my words, Keith ain't always like this.

I suppose Lurlene's jilting him last season cut him to the quick. Hasn't been the same since."

Amanda angled a glance at Lord Saville, who was carrying Lurlene's sunshade while she—with wails and shrieks incorporating the words "mice" and "horrid snakes"— tiptoed through the grass toward a group of folding chairs. His brows were pulled up in amusement and his lips were wreathed in smiles. Sitting down next to Lurlene, he bent closer to her and whispered something in her ear. She preened and cooed.

Flanked by Sir Anthony and Pamela, the Dowager was tottering along the path in the opposite direction.

"I believe there are some stone benches around that curve, and if we can only make it there, we'll have a respite. I'm afraid I ain't a country person," Sir Digby said grimly, as he gingerly stepped along the path, his face already puce from the heat of the midday sun.

They reached the dubious comfort of a stone bench without mishaps, and Sir Digby breathed easier. "I'll have to rest for a moment before venturing back. This air is very potent, and I'm working up a great appetite." He smacked his lips with anticipation. "My lackeys will be serving lobster in aspic—refreshing on a hot day like this, don't you think? Poached salmon, cucumber soup, roasted quails and pigeon pies, a mixture of salads, buttered rolls, and for dessert—almond crust tarts with succulent strawberries and clotted cream. Ahh, could you but imagine my passion for clotted cream, Miss Amanda!" He put up one fleshy finger. "Mind you, that ain't all there is to be sampled, but my memory eludes me. Hmm, a few bottles of excellent hock are cooling on ice, of course."

"I hope you won't have one of your heated arguments with Pamela on the advantages of fresh strawberries over jam," Amanda teased with a smile, and plied her fan, hiding a small yawn behind it. The soporific stillness of the park was doing much to calm her nerves. The birds sang in the trees, and two sparrows hopped along the lane to regard them with jeweled eyes.

"We can safely return now that we've done our romantic bit," Sir Digby said with evident relief in his voice. "I think I'll have a tiny snack before lunch. The air is very bracing here, and makes me more famished by the minute."

As she couldn't trust her own treacherous emotions, Amanda had scant desire to come face to face with Lord Saville sooner than necessary. But, with her hand on Sir Digby's sleeve, she adjusted her step to his rolling gait, and as they turned the bend in the path, the sound of voices reached their ears.

Lurlene sat where Lord Saville had left her, now accompanied by the Dowager and the rest of the party except the marquess. Of him there was no sign.

The lackeys were emptying well-filled baskets, placing cutlery and plates, domed silver dishes. crystal glasses, and exquisitely embroidered napkins on the table.

"Why, this is like a regular dining room table moved outdoors," Amanda exclaimed.

Sir Digby sent her an affronted glare. "Well, do you expect us to spread out on the ground? I would need block and tackle to get up if I ever sat down on the grass," he said with evident disgust.

Amanda went pink with mirth. "I needed that snub. You think of everything, Sir Digby."

He seemed pleased at the compliment. "I like to think that I serve a first-class meal—and it certainly wouldn't be if ants were traipsing through the butter and beetles swimming in the sauce boats."

Amanda's eyes twinkled. "Of course. That would be

fairly rustic. Please join the others. I have to fetch my reticule from the landau."

"One of my flunkies can surely oblige," Sir Digby demurred, his face creased with worry.

"Oh, it's no bother at all. In fact, I rather like walking on the grass. I promise I won't trip." She realized he wasn't thinking of her difficulties, but of his own as he began maneuvering his vast frame across the lawn without assistance. He looked slightly ridiculous, his arms extended and fingers spread for balance. His shoe tips tapped the ground suspiciously for treacherous holes.

Amanda skipped to the landau parked in deep shade behind a clump of trees. She was still smiling broadly at the memory of Sir Digby's antics. Sorely in need of a handkerchief to pat the perspiration from her face, she stepped into the carriage to retrieve her reticule. On returning to the ground, a shadow fell over her and Lord Saville's hand shot forth, gripping her wrist. She jumped with bewilderment, a sinking feeling in her stomach.

"Unhand me!" she demanded, in vain trying to pull away from him.

"Well, well, Amanda—did you follow me to take up our business where we stopped last time?" he drawled, his eyes filled with wicked amusement.

"Not at all," she replied coldly. "You must have a very high opinion of yourself to believe that I would come after you, to yet again be mauled and humiliated. No, my lord, never!" With a hard wrench she regained her hand, absently rubbing the spot his fingers had gripped.

He laughed, a deep hearty sound. "You're most delightful, and so *severe*. For your information I came here to check on the horses." Leaning both hands on the top of his cane, he studied her. "And, as usual, I get treated to the rough side of your tongue."

"What do you expect—startling me out of my wits like that?" Amanda's eyes flashed dark fire, and her heart pounded like a mad thing against her ribs. "I shouldn't be talking to you. I don't know what evil game you're playing with Lurlene, but I have no desire to be caught in the middle. If you knew what's best for you, you'd stop hounding her—and me."

His eyes half-closed, he observed her idly. "Another lecture? The Dowager gave me my comeuppance, so you don't have to lash out at me."

Peering into his smoky eyes, Amanda found herself without argument. His eyes made her grow hot and then cold, and her breath choked in her throat. There was something in his gaze that fought her, but also beckoned her. And there was a strength she was powerless to fight.

"I daresay I'm sorry for jumping to the wrong conclusion," she whispered. "Naturally I have no right to judge you, but somehow your words and demeanor always provoke my anger." She managed a small, if wintry, smile.

"There, that's much better. Your smile is like the sun emerging from a bank of clouds." His smoldering glance raked the very bottom of her heart, and she saw—behind the usual surface of arrogance—a deep pain and anger. She sensed that the haughty marquess was lonely, just like herself. A wrenching longing to know more about him, the hidden him, tore through her.

"I suppose we should return to the tables before the Dowager becomes suspicious. I don't want to get short shrift from her again." As he held out his arm, Amanda had no choice but to put her fingers in the crook of his elbow. Butterflies fluttered wildly in her stomach and she chided herself for obeying his command.

CHAPTER 11

As A BANK of pewter-colored clouds moved slowly over the horizon, Sir Digby's guests applied themselves with obvious pleasure to the delicacies on the table. The Dowager, whose appetite was as bird-like as her body, held sway at her end of the table with a running commentary on the latest *on dits* of polite society. Amanda marveled at her knowledge, since the Dowager rarely left her house in South Street.

A lackey placed a plate of lobster in aspic, garnished with a sprig of parsley, before Amanda. Sipping a glass of white wine, she noticed that Pamela was sitting on Sir Digby's other side, holding his entire attention. Amanda was left to her own thoughts. Sir Anthony chattered in her ear, but Amanda heard not a word. She shivered in the sudden cold gust of wind.

Try as she might, Amanda couldn't tear her eyes away from Lord Saville and Lurlene seated on the opposite side of the table. The marquess was plying Lurlene with the choicest of the delicacies, keeping her utterly rapt with his suave attention. A dart of hot jealousy stabbed Amanda's

heart, but she was determined not to lose her enjoyment of
the outing. At that moment Lord Saville's smoky green gaze
pierced hers, causing her breath to grow ragged and her
heart to somersault. She averted her gaze with utmost
difficulty.

Concentrating in vain on the food, Amanda listened
casually to Pamela's and Sir Digby's conversation. The
sound of their voices threaded through her mind, but she did
not hear the words. Pamela's face shone pink with delight as
she listened to Sir Digby's lengthy explanation where to
find the best salmon at the London fishmarket. He looked
much refreshed and totally oblivious to a buzzing fly drawn
by the sweet scent of his hair pomade. His voice rose a little
as he described how to best make turtle soup, and when he
ended, Pamela continued with one of her favorite recipes.
Evidently, the couple had eyes for no one but each other. A
match made in heaven. . . .

Amanda smiled to herself at the prospect of that carping
old horror, Lady Elfina Waring, finding out about Pamela's
instant success in London. What would she think about Sir
Digby as a suitor to her "lamb"? He had the best of
dispositions, and if Pamela could accept his gross figure,
Amanda wasn't going to stand in their way—and no one
else either, she vowed, compressing her lips in determination.

The wind tossed her napkin across the table to land on
Lord Saville's plate. "A penny for your thoughts, Miss
Amanda," she heard his voice through her daydream.

"I don't want to bore you with trivialities, milord," she
answered with a bland smile and a shrug.

"Nothing you say ever bores me," came his gallant
response, words that earned him a hard rap from Lurlene's
fan and a petulant toss of her head.

"Keith, you sly dog! I could almost suspect you of flirting with Amanda."

"By Jove, I think you're right," Lord Saville teased, his eyes ablaze with mischief.

"I see that I'm unwanted here." Lurlene's lips drooped, and Amanda was hard put to conceal her smile when Lurlene forced a perfectly round tear to roll with dramatic slowness down her cheek.

"Don't be a wetgoose," Lord Saville cajoled, "you know how it ruins your complexion, Lurlene."

The Dowager could not suppress a crow of mirth. She was sitting at an angle to Lurlene, hearing every word of the conversation. Her sharp eyes assessed Lord Saville for a moment, and then she admonished, "Impudent young puppy!"

"My sentiment exactly," said Lurlene in deeply wounded tones.

"Perhaps we should take you home to Justin. If my memory serves me right, he has a very good hand with your tantrums," the Dowager said imperatively.

Lurlene pulled in her bottom lip in defiance. "He always puts my desires first," she declared as if such were her rightful due.

"Yes, Lurlene, we know all about that." The Dowager gave the young woman a brisk slap on the back, rolling her eyes heavenward.

Lurlene's face blanched with shock at such unladylike treatment, and she forgot to produce more tears as she stared open-mouthed at her mother-in-law.

Before Lurlene could go into hysterics, everyone's attention was diverted as a burgundy and gold barouche drew up, wheels crunching the gravel. Down stepped Lord Wrexham, who solicitously helped his partner, Lady Olivia

Lexington, to alight. Then he assisted her mother, the Marchioness of Lexington.

"Ah! Looks like Wrexham is really serious about Lady Olivia. We may expect an announcement soon. He's a lucky fellow," commented Lord Saville *sotto voce*.

Lurlene had turned waxen, and two bright red spots glared on her cheekbones. "What is that *woman* doing here?" she demanded in a carrying staccato voice.

"Mind your manners!" ordered the Dowager. "What has gotten into you? This is a public park, after all."

"Livvy tried to ruin my life once," Lurlene complained, which caused Lord Saville to glance at her in speculation. "I do not wish to share the park with her."

Filled with exasperation, Amanda observed Lurlene's sudden flare of hatred. "Don't fly into the boughs over nothing, Lurlene. Collect yourself!" she scolded. She wished that her father had chosen a lady like Olivia, a hundredfold nicer person than her stepmother, but there was no accounting for tastes.

"Look at her costume," Lurlene continued in a peevish whisper, mauling Lord Saville's sleeve. "She wore that ridiculous hat in Hyde Park last week. She's so *common*, despite her title."

"Be that as it may. I think she looks ravishing," Amanda said with snappy emphasis on the last word.

Lady Olivia did; her statuesque red-gold beauty and creamy skin was complemented by a pale-green sarcenet walking ensemble with matching hat set at a rakish angle on her short curls.

Lord Saville looked utterly bored, but he rose and bowed as the beauty and her entourage passed by. They waved cheerfully before setting up their picnic farther down by the river—the Thames, flowing languidly through the green paradise of Richmond.

Lurlene sat through the encounter with a rigid back, her eyes dilated with venom. She made no gesture to return Lady Olivia's pleasant greeting. Amanda was convinced Lurlene's animosity stemmed from the fact that Lady Olivia was quite as lovely, if not lovelier, than Lurlene. Her stepmother couldn't stand any kind of competition.

To rub salt in the wound, the Dowager gave a snort and turned to Lurlene. "That fine filly puts us all in the shade with such abundance of *dignity*," she said, her tone of voice implying that her daughter-in-law lacked such refinement. It was true, but needed not be weathered abroad, Amanda thought with an irate stare at her grandmother.

The stormy spell was broken when Sir Digby's lackeys brought forward a tray laden with strawberry tarts. Even though the wind was wreaking havoc on tablecloth and napkins, they began to distribute the dessert, and Lurlene's sore temper calmed as a tart was set before her. She immediately spooned a large mound of whipped cream on top of the berries.

Lord Saville bent a thoughtful gaze to his plate, and Amanda wondered what had caused the deep crease between his eyebrows. She couldn't know that he was pondering the reason for Lurlene's exaggerated anger, and the connection between Lady Olivia and Lord Bowen. He vaguely remembered a rumor that Lord Bowen had planned to marry Livvy. Drawing a sigh of relief, he considered himself lucky to have escaped Lurlene. Her presence suffocated him, and Amanda's trim figure and frank face on the other side of the table was a solace and delight to his tortured mind.

In fact, he could easily picture himself living with a woman like Amanda. Love would soften her thorny character. A wave of warmth rose in his chest. He would like to be the man she loved, he realized with a jolt. As Dig leaned over to squeeze Amanda's hand, he was jerked back to reality. Amanda would become his uncle's wife; never his. He had to curb his emotions, forget the attraction.

Taking a deep breath, he said, "Lurlene, would you like to take a walk? I believe there is a passably smooth path along the river."

"Ihhh," Lurlene shrieked. "You don't know what creatures lurk in the grass—for all I know there could be poisonous spiders." She fluttered her hands in front of her face. "I feel faint at the thought of such torment. Keith, how could you be so heartless to even suggest such a thing?"

"I believe the peasants walk *barefoot* more often than not—and none the worse for it," Saville said tonelessly, but a smile tugged at the corners of his lips.

Lurlene shuddered. "What a horrifying thought that *I* should behave like a peasant. Why, you're a walking monument of inconsideration!"

"Really? I didn't suggest you walk barefoot, surely. I thought you took pleasure in my company and would do anything for me, Lurlene."

Her eyes were stormy and mutinous. "Not even for Justin will I take off my shoes outdoors." She pouted and clamped a possessive hand over Lord Saville's arm. "I do like your company, and I beg you not to leave my side—I need the strength of a man in this unpredictable environment."

"You will not be without male protection." With finality Lord Saville pried loose her petrified grip, and turned to Amanda. "Are you afraid of the Richmond 'wilds,' Miss Bowen?"

Amused by Lurlene's affectations, Amanda hesitated for a moment. "No, but I don't think a walk is a good idea." She pointed at the lowering sky. "We'll be drenched ere long."

"By Jupiter, you're right. We'd better take refuge at

some inn," Sir Digby said with disappointment. "We'll never make it back to London before the rain."

"I will die of inflammation of the lungs, mark my words, and it will be on your conscience," Lurlene whined, swatting Lord Saville's arm with her fan.

"Calm yourselves," Sir Digby admonished testily. "No one is going to come to any harm." He stood with difficulty. "My party has been ruined just as we were having the most pleasant of conversations." He beamed at Pamela before ordering his lackeys to pack everything and head back to London.

Nervously fingering the hem of his waistcoat, he contemplated the distance between the table and the carriage. Then he offered Lady Pamela his arm. "Shall we?"

Like a majestic ship, he swayed across the grass, followed by the others. Amanda placed her shawl across her grandmother's shoulders and led her to the barouche. Sir Digby had had the foresight to bring some rugs, just in case the weather changed. More often than not it did, especially in the spring.

The Dowager grumbled about looking like a sausage when Lord Saville had tucked two rugs around her. It was a subdued party that left the once-sunny glade by the Thames. Lord Wrexham and Lady Olivia had canceled their picnic before it even began. Their carriage left in the opposite direction.

"Good riddance to them," Lurlene said. "At least we don't have to spend the rest of the afternoon cramped in some small tavern in their company."

Just as they left the park, the first raindrops fell. The rain was carried on a cold wind toward London. The lovely morning was only a memory now.

They stopped at the first inn on the road to town. The rain was falling heavily as the ladies hurried inside the small tavern. A fire blazed in the stone fireplace and the plank floor was wet with recent scrubbing. The low-ceilinged room smelled of ale and burnt meat.

"What a god-awful place," Lurlene said in a loud whisper just as the host stepped forward.

Amanda nudged her in the ribs. "Don't start, Lurlene. A cup of tea before the fire will cheer you up."

The host looked pleased at the prospect of serving the Quality, and embarked on a discussion of the inn's fare with Sir Digby. Amanda led the Dowager to the fire and they warmed their hands before sitting down on a settle to await fairer weather.

"It smells in here," Lurlene went on. "It makes me quite nauseated."

"Oh, go on with you, I'm certain you'll survive this afternoon without scars," said the Dowager. Then she turned to Amanda and asked her to send Sir Digby to fetch her shawl from the carriage.

Lurlene held up her skirt as she gingerly sat on the edge of a wingchair. "There must be all sorts of *insects* and other vermin here."

"I'll go, Grandmama. Sir Digby is occupied at the moment." Amanda stood. "Can you stay here alone with Lurlene until the gentlemen join us?" she whispered to the Dowager.

"While you're away, Mandy, I'll see to it that Lurlene won't be devoured by a"—the Dowager thought for a moment, her lips widening in a crafty smile—"a big hairy *spider*."

Lurlene let out a wail that could have put a banshee to shame, and clapped her hands to her ears. "How c-cruel of you, Mama!" she sobbed, and hurtled herself onto Sir Anthony's scrawny chest as he joined them by the fire.

"That was very naughty, Grandmama—and indeed uncalled for," Amanda berated.

"An old cat like me is entitled to a few jokes," the Dowager defended herself stoutly. "Especially after being dragged bodily from the comforts of my own home to suffer the company of certain *persons*."

"I daresay," Amanda said in her driest tone. "But if you recall, you pushed yourself uninvited into this." She escaped before the Dowager could make an acid rejoinder. There was no sign of Lord Saville, and Lady Pamela was hanging on Sir Digby's arm as he ordered tea and brandy from the host.

Holding a rug over her head, Amanda braved the weather and darted to the stables around the side of the half-timbered inn. The barouche had been pulled through the wide door into the dark interior of a barn. The ramshackle building smelled of old dusty straw.

The rain whispered on the thatched roof and splashed off the eaves to the ground. Amanda's feet were wet as she reached the interior. She was shocked to find Lord Saville sitting on one of the seats, massaging his leg. He was quite white around the lips. As he became aware of her presence, he forced out a smile.

"Are you in pain?" she asked, sensing his struggle.

"Nothing that signifies," he said, but his voice was flat with misery. "Deadly sort of picnic, don't you agree?"

Amanda nodded and reached inside the carriage for the Dowager's shawl. "Yes, disastrous." She peered at the blue-gray clouds. "I hope it will blow over soon."

"Come, let me show you something." With difficulty, Lord Saville stepped down and led her toward the back of the barn. There were wide gaps between the planks and he pointed to them. "Look through there."

Amanda was surprised to find that the river was flowing

behind the inn. Weeping willows touched the water with feathery fronds and created a silent green dome above the river. A pair of swans glided slowly by, their necks arched, beaks close to the water, eyes alert, in search of edible algae in the murky depths. Except for the plop of raindrops on the water, serene stillness reigned.

"How lovely," she whispered. She didn't dare to look at Lord Saville, fearing that her eyes would betray her feelings. One look from him could ruin her fragile composure. They admired the view in silence for a few minutes, absorbing the scent of wet earth and bark.

"This reminds me of my country seat, Ashborough Castle—the fragrant air, the silence, the subtle changing of the seasons," Lord Saville said so close to her ear that she could feel his breath.

Amanda peeked at him from under her eyelashes. She felt a mercurial leap of spirits. "Sometimes, after a ride in the park or a walk, I long to return to the country."

"By Jove! You never cease to amaze me, Amanda. I thought young ladies of quality had no further interest than continuous entertainment and fripperies."

Amanda shrugged. "The balls are all the same, the tattlemongers ruthless, and one always has to guard one's tongue."

The marquess chuckled. "I've never seen you pay any heed to that before, Miss Amanda. I find your frankness quite refreshing—a change from the regular collection of simpering misses and peabrains with nothing in their heads but wedding gowns and bells."

"Milord, it rankles to hear you talk in that unfair vein about ladies. I believe females have lots of interests besides balls and the latest fashions."

He sighed. "When I'm with you, I always put my foot in

my mouth. You have that effect on me. I repeatedly forget your serious turn of mind. I'm sorry."

Amanda slewed her eyes toward his face, startled by his apology. Was he really honest, or was it yet another taste of his sarcastic taunts?

"Your conversation always borders on the improper; I never know what to make of it."

He gripped her elbow, his face earnest. "I meant every word. Some day, Amanda, I'd like to show you Ashborough Castle. If you like history, I'm certain you'll appreciate the old heap of stones. I can almost hear the steps of William the Conqueror's soldiers ring out on the uneven stone floor. It's an enormous legacy, and the upkeep is important," he said with proud passion. "I'm always busy with restorations—an avocation of mine."

"Lord Saville, Ashborough Castle sounds like a place of enchantment." She smiled. "I will tell you a secret even though you might call me a blue-stocking. History has always fascinated me. I read all the books I can find on the subject."

"I should have known." He relaxed his hold on her elbow and stepped away from her, as if suddenly recalling the impropriety of the situation. He cleared his throat. "We'll have to discuss our mutual interest some time. And please dispense with my title. Without preamble I've called you Amanda these many days." An engaging twinkle accompanied his words, and Amanda drowned in the depths of his smoky eyes so close to her own. Through the wall planks, daylight played on his head, tempting her to bury her fingers into his glossy hair. She wanted to close the distance between them, to once again feel the warm caress of his lips on hers. An odd sensation, which she could only call an urgent craving for his touch, prodded her impatiently.

"Very well, but I don't know if we should become that

familiar—to discuss history, I mean," she said. Her voice sounded so far away, fuzzy around the edges, and all she could think of was the bold curve of his lips.

He wrenched away, and flung out his arm in exasperation. "You're right! If I know old Dig right, he's on the verge of offering for you. I don't want to put a spoke in the wheel. We can discuss history later, when that matter is settled." His voice was gritty. "Nevertheless, you can't deny that we've become increasingly familiar."

Amanda blushed and averted her gaze. The mention of Sir Digby's name brought her back to earth in a hurry. She debated whether to tell Lord Saville the truth, but decided against it. It was up to Sir Digby to divulge their secret pact to his nephew. What a muddle!

The marquess drew closer again, and Amanda could feel the firm strength of his biceps against her shoulder. She could not bear to pull away from him, although decorum dictated a certain space between them.

"You know, I rather envy my uncle," he pronounced suddenly.

Her breath faltered momentarily from the shock of his words. "What do you mean?" A river of pure pleasure surged through her as he placed his arm casually around her shoulders.

"Just what I said. Old Dig is fortunate to have your affection, and I know you'll make him a splendid wife." He heaved a sigh. "There it is—I've cleared my breast." He smiled wryly. "Dare I hope for your friendship although we've bickered a lot in the past?"

Amanda made a gesture of defeat and sighed. "Yes, perhaps. . . ." She felt a rush of color flood her face, and almost confessed that she had no intention whatsoever to marry Sir Digby when he, Saville, held her love.

"I quite like our verbal battles, and I pray they won't stop now. You're highly entertaining," he said.

Amanda fanned her face vigorously. "Like the clown Grimaldi? Perhaps I should stand on my head, or perform a few cartwheels. Oh, Keith, you're exaggerating." She liked the sound of his name on her lips—so solid. "I'm indeed a dull, conventional person. I have a passion for embroidery, and I have a shocking partiality to romantic novels. I have to hide them under the pillows away from Grandmama's eagle eye, but I strongly suspect she reads them when I'm out."

His lips curved. "She would do that, of course." He casually dropped his arm from her shoulder. A sigh slid over his lips. "It fascinates me to hear details about your life—in fact, everything about you fascinates me," he whispered, forgetting that he had no right to make love to his uncle's bride-to-be.

"Even my unfashionable coloring?" Amanda asked shyly, once more losing herself in the deep pools of his eyes.

"Your hair is like the finest black silk, and I'd like to push my fingers through it." His gaze caressed her curls for one breathless moment. "And your eyes are bottomless obsidian—inscrutable, with flashes of red light when you're angry. Your skin invites a man's touch."

Amanda chuckled. "Roguish, knavish words, Keith! Is this how you make debutantes fall to your feet?" She tried to make her voice flippant, but a tiny tremble betrayed her inner turmoil. His lips beckoned, only inches from hers, and the subtle scent of his shaving soap seduced her senses. A watery ray of sunshine pulled out the shifting sea-color of his eyes—mercurial, hypnotic. The moment stretched eternal and she sank deeper in his spell, but his lips never reached hers. The tip of his thumb tickled her chin, bringing her slowly back to reality.

The enchantment torn, he pulled away. "How remiss of me to keep you out here for a bit of flirting." His voice had regained its usual light sarcastic tint, but a flash of uncertainty clouded his face.

Amanda carefully hid her own feelings. She wrinkled her forehead. "I recall a moment when you called me 'a righteous little bagpipe,' or something like that."

He barked a laugh, his head thrown back. "Coin for coin, my dear! That was for 'top-lofty ignorant.'"

Amanda delivered a stern glance, but it could not be maintained under his dancing eyes. "I see. But then it was double revenge. I clearly remember that your retribution came in the form of a ruthless kiss."

He smote his chest with a tragic air. "Aye, and the punishment was all mine! The boldness of your lips drenched my heart with sweetness." He began reeling as if in a drunken stupor.

"Desist, do!" she admonished with a soft laugh. "I don't know what tomfoolery has assailed you, but it won't fadge. We have to return to the inn, and Grandmama will certainly give you a setdown if you display further whimsy."

"A shocking prospect." An unholy gleam shone in his eyes. He cleared his throat, donning a slightly pompous mask, and straightened his back severely. "Is this better?"

"Much better." She stepped back, turning her back on him. "As you well know, the only cause to our arguments is Lurlene. I have one tiny wish—that you'd leave my stepmother alone. There must be any number of ladies ready to fall at your feet. Besides, I don't believe your professed adoration is the only reason you follow Lurlene around. There is something else."

"Lord Bowen should be proud of such a loyal—and

perceptive—daughter, but I'm not at all sure that Lurlene deserves such a staunch defender," he responded cryptically.

A sudden cold wind blew between them.

"I don't understand," Amanda breathed, sensing that she was on the verge of finding out something he so carefully kept hidden.

He shrugged and gave a dry chuckle. "You'll understand sooner or later." Veering away from the sensitive issue of Lurlene, he said, "I'm glad we're friends. Old Digby will be delighted to hear that we've buried the hatchet."

"We should be going back," she said, her voice strangely hoarse. She wanted to be more than friends, so much more.

CHAPTER 12

JUST AS AMANDA THOUGHT that her relation with Lord
Saville had turned more intimate, he began courting Lurlene
with renewed vigor. Amanda was crushed and angry with
herself for ever weakening to his charm. She had fallen like
a stone. She was glad that Sir Digby kept up their charade
of a relationship without telling Lord Saville the truth about
their pact.

It was obvious that Pamela took more and more pleasure
in Sir Digby's company. The couple had ample opportunity
to meet while Sir Digby, all through the month of May,
doggedly maintained the appearance of courting Amanda.

Amanda couldn't understand his reluctance to accept his
feelings for Pamela, and he never suggested that the pact
should be broken. Society was abuzz with conjecture, the
gentlemen betting in the clubs as to what date the shy Sir
Digby was going to come up to scratch and offer for
Amanda. There came a time when it could not be delayed
further without raising excessive speculation, but the gam-
blers didn't know that fate held a quirk in store, voiding all
bets.

During one of his morning calls, Amanda pressed Sir Digby to make his tender feelings known to Pamela. She divulged that she had told Pamela the truth, so there was no need fearing her shock at the subterfuge. Sir Digby looked flushed and bothered.

"She'll expect matrimony, and I shudder at the thought of so great a step," he said plaintively as they were momentarily alone in the green salon in South Street.

"Besides getting a loving wife, you would benefit financially from a marriage to Pamela. I take it you haven't found another way to gain access to your inheritance?" Amanda went on inexorably.

He squirmed under her daunting gaze. "No—not really," he admitted, his face a series of gloomy folds.

"Well, there you are. You have to marry *somebody*, and since you get along splendidly with Pamela, you two have to make a match of it. I might as well go as far as assuming that you're in love with her." Amanda paid no heed to the shock on his face. Studying the intricate embroidery in the frame in front of her, she waited a few moments to let her words sink in. "I'm certain she wouldn't be averse to a proposal."

He nervously patted his curls and groaned. "You must be bamming me. This is all too sudden. I need more time." He gulped at the frightening prospect of marrying Lady Pamela. As if desperately clutching at straws, he said, "What about you, Miss Amanda? You'll be at the mercy of the Dowager. She won't hesitate to choose a husband for you when she finds out the truth about us."

Amanda pulled her eyebrows together in a frown. "Yes, I suppose you're right." Then she shrugged. "However, you approach Pamela and we'll make an agreement to keep mum about your betrothal until the end of the season. That will give you more time to *think*—and me time to escape from London. An odd couple we make!" she added with a sudden smile, provoking him to laugh. His huge body rippled, the buttons of his waistcoat threatening to pop.

"I agree. Quite a situation we have created," he said when he had regained his breath. "A plot that devil's spawn, Keith, could have devised. Nothing is beyond him, you know. But, like you said, I'm sure we'll manage to keep the Dowager—and the rest of the world—in the dark for a few more weeks."

When Amanda later spoke with Pamela, the reaction was what she had expected. Pamela's eyes lit up and her cheeks suffused with color. Seeing Pamela's dreamy expression, Amanda knew she was doing the right thing by pushing the star-struck, if excruciatingly shy, couple along.

"I believe you'd suit admirably," she said with much confidence. "But do you fully accept his—ahem, figure? You won't be able to change his ways, you know that, don't you, Pam?"

"Yes, of course, his foremost passion is food, after all. But I have never met a *kinder* gentleman; he always treats me with consideration and such style."

Amanda vented the worry closest to her heart. "What about Great-aunt Elfina? Will she approve of the match?"

"Honestly, I don't know." Pamela made a dismissing gesture with her hands. "But I'm out of her clutches now, so what does it matter?"

Amanda decided the best road was one of brutal sincerity. "She might try to ruin your happiness out of spite. Do you really want to make a connection of which she disapproves?"

Lady Pamela fretted much in the same way Sir Digby had, but not for fear of matrimony. "Of course not, but I think I—love him, and the old lady might understand that."

Amanda made a noise of disgust. "Humbug! She only

wants you to make a prestigious marriage, my dear. Love does not come into the picture." Then she smiled. "But together we'll handle her, somehow. Trust me, I have had ample practice with Grandmama."

Pamela looked doubtful, and Amanda found her patience sorely tried one week later as her plan went awry.

As Billings admitted a pale and perspiring Sir Digby to the house in South Street, she happened to come down the curving staircase in the hallway. Taking one look at his agitated mien, she knew why he had come.

Sir Digby stood on the doorstep with a bunch of fragrant hothouse roses clutched in his hand. He was dressed impeccably in tight fawn pantaloons, a coat of blue superfine, and a white satin waistcoat with gold-plated buttons. Fobs and seals dangled from a gold chain across his paunch.

Amanda urgently demanded some time alone with him before he entered the green salon where the Dowager was receiving morning callers. She maintained, in a low intense voice, that the Dowager was bound to find out his errand, since he carried flowers and wore such a sober face.

"Have you already forgotten our decision not to spread the news until the end of the season?" she asked.

He shook his head and looked guilty. But the flash of guilt disappeared rapidly from his moon-face, and he waved her testily away. "I spent the entire night pacing the floor of my lodgings dredging up courage to approach Lady Pamela. It's now or never. I've never been more agitated in my life!" he said with a grim tremble on his voice. "You don't know what agony I've lived through these last twenty-four hours. Proposing is worse than the worst toothache. I'm awfully sorry, but I can't go through such horror one more night." He waddled toward the door, clenching the flowers with a shaking hand.

"Very well," Amanda sighed, "good luck then." She

should have known this was coming. How would she ever explain this to her grandmother? When the Dowager found out the truth, her matchmaking efforts would be renewed with gale force. Amanda would have to find a new way to evade her grandmother now that Sir Digby had broken their pact. "Sir Digby, old wretch," she whispered, and followed in his wake.

That particular morning, Lady Pamela looked her best in a pale rose muslin gown drawn tightly under her large bosom with a darker velvet ribbon, a spray of velvet pansies attached to the décolletage. A silver rouleau threaded through her gentle curls. Her eyes sparkled and her cheeks blossomed rosy with excitement as soon as she laid eyes on Sir Digby.

He ambled into the green salon, and the Dowager gave him a mistrustful glance. Then she stared narrowly at Amanda, following closely behind him. "What's afoot?" she asked querulously. "I take it that wilted bouquet is not for me."

Sir Digby blushed and inserted a finger between his collar and neck. "I—ahem, the flowers are for Lady Pamela," he said, and held out the roses with a trembling hand.

Pamela accepted the bouquet readily and buried her nose in its sweet fragrance. "How thoughtful of you, Sir Digby." She smiled encouragingly, and he found the mettle to clear his throat and come to the point.

"Lady Bowen," he said to the Dowager, blanching as the Bowen black look bored into him. "I—er—well, you see, I would like to speak with Lady Pamela alone for a few minutes, if you don't mind."

"Whatever for?" the Dowager demanded imperiously.

"Have something very important to tell her, y'see." Sir Digby seemed to grow with importance as he gazed lovingly at Lady Pamela.

"Very well, you may have five minutes, but if you try

some tomfoolery, I'll have a strip of your hide, young man!"

She rose with a regal air and pinned Amanda with an awful look. Amanda assisted her grandmother out of the room and closed the door. But before she could open her mouth to explain, the old tartar had pressed her ear shamelessly to the keyhole.

Sir Digby's booming voice could easily be heard through the wood, and Amanda flinched, trying to wrest her grandmother into another salon. "Come, Grandmama, Pam will tell us all about this later."

The Dowager shrugged her off. "Let go, gel. This will be entertaining." Her ear connected once more with the wood.

There was the alarming sound of creaking corsets, and Amanda deduced that Sir Digby had somehow managed to get down on one knee. He sounded tortured as he lost himself in a string of inanities before coming to the issue closest to his heart. "I know I should beg permission from Lady Waring as your closest relative before paying my addresses to you, Lady Pamela, but I sorely need to find out your true, ahem—feelings for me first. I've lived in agony of this moment." A groan of despair could be heard. "I—I now ask—beg you—on my—er, knees, to become my wife." Then he frantically added, "But don't be afraid to turn down my offer if it's distasteful to you, dearest Lady Pamela."

The Dowager gasped, and her eyes bulged. She tottered to the adjoining small anteroom and collapsed on the nearest chair. "I've never—"

"There, there," soothed Amanda, searching her grandmother's reticule for a vinaigrette. She held it under the Dowager's pale jutting nose.

The old woman struggled to sit up straight, brandishing her arms. "You—you were the one he— *What* is that dashed coxcomb about?" she demanded dourly, desperately inhaling the sharp vinegar. "It's all your fault, Mandy! You're forcing me to an early grave."

"Nonsense! Don't get rough with me, Grandmama. You must have noticed their growing affection. Surely it cannot come as such a big surprise to you," Amanda said innocently, mentally cursing Sir Digby for his haste. "I wish them all the happiness in the world."

The Dowager muttered something unintelligible and glowered at Amanda from under her bristly bar of eyebrows. "Miss, I know that guileless air of yours! I don't understand what havey-cavey business you're involved in, but mark my words, you've just lost your only chance for a decent marriage." Her anger gusted with every word. "I had hoped for another suitor for you, but since no other gentleman has showed any particular interest, I had to bow to the inevitable and accept Sir Digby as your only road to wedded bliss. He *is* very plump in the pocket and a *manageable* sort of fellow. Mandy, I shudder to find out what you've done to turn Sir Digby against you."

Amanda laughed in exasperation, and flung herself onto a sofa. "Oh, Grandmama, you're incorrigible—always suspicious. But this time *I* didn't do a thing. Sir Digby had his own idea of happiness. You're just going to have to accept Dig's change of bridal candidates." She added a small lie. "I told him I didn't want to marry him."

"Is that so, miss!" The Dowager mimicked Amanda's airy tones. " 'Twill be difficult to digest this new turn of events for an old lady like me, you know. I was quite set on this match for you."

Amanda waggled a censoring finger. "You'll have to hold your tongue, Grandmama. It won't do to rake Pamela over the coals for this. Today is bound to be the happiest day of her life."

The Dowager made a grunt of reluctant agreement, and struggled to her feet. "Yes, if she accepts Sir Digby's offer, she has more sense than you'll ever have. Too bad she had her eyes on your beau. I'll be left with an aging spinster on my hands by the end of the season," she said in a calculated broken voice, but Amanda was untouched.

"I am not yet in my dotage, Grandmama. And where are you going now?" she demanded.

"To my bedchamber to write Elfina a letter which will carry some explosive news to my sister." Cackling, the Dowager hastened toward the door with renewed vigor.

Amanda sighed. "I'm sure Sir Digby would like to write to her before you do. You know how Great-aunt Elfina is. She'll run amok at Waring Manor if she hears about this from you first."

"Bibble-babble!" the Dowager rejoined, and closed the door behind her with a slam. Amanda knew it was useless to argue further.

Sir Digby and Pamela emerged from the green salon, a happy light in their eyes. Sir Digby looked inordinately proud. He cleared his throat to speak. "Miss Pamela has consented to become my wife," he said in awed tones, but with a beaming countenance.

"Thank God! I knew you would get up the pluck to ask her, sooner or later." Silently Amanda wished it had been later. "I'm filled with unspeakable delight. This calls for a toast, and I think you should hurry to write to Lady Waring—this very minute!"

The next day was Wednesday, anxiously awaited by Lurlene as the day of the promised necklace.

Lord Saville scrawled a note to be attached to a package on the desk in front of him. The parcel's destination was

Lady Olivia Lexington's townhouse in Curzon Street. She was one to appreciate a good joke, he hoped.

Calling in a footman rigged out in the splendid Saville livery of ice-blue satin with silver braiding and powdered tie wig, the marquess ordered him to deliver the box. He stressed the importance of giving it straight into Lady Olivia's hand. Counting on that lady's vanity, he held no doubt that his gift would be displayed that evening, just as he had indicated on the card.

Having dispatched his messenger, the marquess leaned back in his leather wingchair with a satisfied smile on his lips. This action would create a small scandal. He would always savor this day in his memory, his sweet revenge, and tomorrow he could go on with his life and never look at Lurlene again.

The first thing he would do after his revenge was to find out Dig's intentions toward Amanda. Dig was certainly taking his time; was he ever going to propose? Unease rolled through the marquess. He had urged his uncle to choose Amanda for his bride, and now he worried it had been a dreadful mistake. Guilt stabbed through him as he thought of his uncle's slim chances at attracting a female. If Amanda would accept Digby, then he certainly wouldn't stand in their way.

Lurlene had made him bitter, but Amanda had soothed that bitterness, had made him climb out of his pit of misery. He wished he could have forgiven Lurlene for her callous behavior, but it still rankled deeply. He was convinced that she would become all the better for the events about to unfold shortly.

With a deep sigh, he heaved himself out of the chair to place himself in the efficient care of his valet. Even though his leg ached savagely, tonight he would look his best. Perhaps he would even dance.

* * *

Amanda also harbored a desire to look her best, although Almack's was not her choice of where to spend an interesting evening. While she let her curls be tugged from one side to the other by the stalwart Meg, who was in search of a new way to arrange her hair, she thought about the prestigious club in King Street—the only one where females were admitted.

Several high-ranking patronesses ruled Almack's with an iron fist, among them Lady Jersey, the icy Mrs. Drummond-Burrell, and Countess Lieven. The waltz was grudgingly allowed, if frowned upon. The refreshments consisted of weak tea and biscuits; and, to the disgust of the male guests, no stronger beverage than ratafia was served. The gentlemen were forced to appear in full evening attire with the universally disliked satin knee-breeches and white silk stockings. Nobody arriving later than eleven o'clock would be permitted past the hallowed portals.

To obtain a voucher to Almack's was tricky at best. Such an honor was bestowed by the approval of at least one patroness, and then only to persons moving in the most elevated circles.

A dead bore, Amanda thought with a sigh.

"I'd like you to place that bandeau around my forehead, like we tried at first," she ordered her impatient maid. She studied her face critically in the mirror above the dressing table, and saw that the paleness and the dark smudges under her eyes became accentuated by the silver-cloth. "No, better still—put it aside."

"Good riddance to the bad rubbish!" Meg exploded, hands on ample hips. "Gawd, miss, this shilly-shallying makes my head spin. I've a good mind to let you dress yourself, Miss Amanda—and a proper mull you'd make of it!"

In spite of Meg's belligerent threat, Amanda was soon dressed in a pale mauve silk shift topped with a Grecian lace tunic. Delicate lace bordered the modest décolletage and also edged the short sleeves. A lace ribbon held together with a silver clasp under her small breasts formed the attractive empire line. The silk whispered gently as she moved, enhancing the lithe slenderness of her body. A thin silver filigree chain embraced her neck, and two ornate silver combs held her curls in place.

Radiant, Pamela pirouetted into the room. She was dressed in a white muslin gown and pearls, and her eyes were soft like dark velvet. She still hasn't come down from the clouds, Amanda thought, knowing that Sir Digby's proposal had prompted her friend's continuous high spirits.

"I can't wait to see Almack's. I'm sure this evening will place every previous event in the shade," Pamela breathed.

"You're heading for a sharp disappointment," Amanda said dampeningly, recalling the gloomy salons at the club. "And remember, you're not allowed to waltz until you get the nod from one of the patronesses." She pursed her lips in thought. "Lady Jersey is your best bet, or Lady Cowper— they aren't as starchy as the rest."

Nothing could squash Lady Pamela's high spirits, not even the Dowager's acid comments as Billings helped her into the carriage. "I'm too old for this, and Almack's is the last place I'd like to be tonight," she murmured and studied her charges with a sharp eye. "But I cannot leave you in the haphazard care of Lurlene. She's bound to bungle your first night there," she said to Pamela with a hint of rough kindness. Pamela kissed the old papery cheek in a fit of enthusiasm.

"Thank you, Great-aunt Ambrosia. I'm convinced that nothing can go wrong in your presence."

"Fiddlesticks!" Pinching Pamela's chin none too gently,

the Dowager warned, "Those high spirits are very well in private, but so *vulgar* in polite society. You have to restrain yourself."

"Admit it, Grandmama, you're only worried she smeared the rouge on your cheek," Amanda cut in.

"Saucy minx," wheezed the Dowager between chuckles that set her purple ostrich feathers bobbing. "At least Pamela has a *reason* to be ebullient—engaged that she is, and to *your* intended."

Pamela's face fell momentarily. "I'm so terribly sorry—"

"She's more than welcome to Sir Digby," Amanda interrupted, straightening the folds of her cloak.

"Bah! If that is so, perhaps you should wangle an invitation to live with *them* after they're married. I've had enough of your sauciness, Mandy," the Dowager said with an indignant toss of plumes, but relented instantly upon seeing Amanda's head droop with sadness. She cleared her throat noisily. "I couldn't resist the opportunity to roast you, granddaughter. None is more pleased with your company than I am."

Amanda could not trust her voice to speak. How could she confide in her grandmother the depression enfolding her? Would her ancient relative understand the painful love she suffered in her heart for the *dastardly* Lord Saville?

There was no more time to brood over her predicament as the carriage pulled up in front of Almack's.

The entrance was crowded with guests, but the Dowager poked a few gentlemen hard with her cane to gain an instant avenue to the door. Well-known and intimidating that she was, the steps cleared as if by a miracle. Soon after greeting the haughty patronesses in the hall, Amanda found herself sitting along the ballroom wall with the other female guests.

The Dowager hissed, quite audibly, that the cakes looked like they were leftovers from last Wednesday, and that the tea had surely boiled for hours. Amanda flinched, frowning darkly at her unruly relative.

Half an hour later, Lurlene made a magnificent entrance on Lord Bowen's arm. She was wearing a narrow gown of sapphire-blue silk, shot with silver threads and trimmed with darker blue bands around the deep décolletage and at the hem. A gold-tasseled white gauze scarf embroidered with blue dots graced her shoulders. Diamonds glittered in her hair, but her throat was as yet unadorned, and Amanda knew very well the reason. A hot flood of anger surged through her. She hated the thought of Keith making a cake of himself before Lurlene and the rest of polite society by presenting her the infamous necklace.

"Ah! There you are," Lord Bowen said with a pleasant smile. He kissed Amanda on the cheek. "You look ravishing as usual, dear Mandy."

A small pout instantly formed on Lurlene's lips as she resented sharing her husband's affection with anyone, even his daughter. But as soon as Justin's gaze returned to her, she smiled sweetly. "Mandy looks very well indeed, but don't you think we should greet the other guests?" As she was pulling his arm, he could only give Amanda an apologetic smile and leave.

Pamela and Amanda exchanged grimaces behind widespread silk fans, but Pamela's attention was soon riveted to the door where Sir Digby and Lord Saville appeared. A slow flush crept above Sir Digby's high collar when he recognized them. In his unique way he plodded across the floor toward them, but Lord Saville remained standing by the door, where Lurlene accosted him. He raised his eyeglass and his green gaze scorched Amanda once, making her heart jolt uncomfortably in her chest, and her breath choke in her throat.

Sir Digby made a handsome bow and beamed at Pamela,

but did not single her out immediately. The gossip—most likely instigated by the Dowager—about the surprising betrothal, was sweeping the *beau monde* like wildfire. Many eyes were aimed in their direction, hoping to witness some discomfort among the trio involved. Amanda could almost feel the calculating minds going full speed behind the false smiles of the most notorious scandalmongers, and she silently approved of Sir Digby's easy grace.

"The two loveliest ladies here tonight," he said. Pursing his lips, he cast an assessing glance around the room. "Yes, definitely quite the loveliest."

"Ha!" the Dowager bellowed. "Don't approve of us old prunes, eh?" She stabbed him in his paunch with her fan. Deeply unsettled, he mopped his face. Amanda came to his aid.

"He was just about to pay his respects, Grandmama, but if you go on in this vein, I'm convinced he'll take his leave in a hurry," she warned coldly.

"Silly young whipstraws, the lot!" the Dowager peeved. "It was different in my heyday—when gentlemen knew how to be truly gallant."

From the corner of her eye, Amanda observed that Lord Saville and Lurlene exited the room together, arms entwined. The corroding fingers of jealousy clawed Amanda's heart. She lost interest in the set forming on the dance floor as she anxiously awaited their return. Keeping the door under constant surveillance, she must have been one of the first to notice Lady Olivia Lexington entering on the arm of Lord Wrexham. Amanda couldn't recall a time when Olivia had looked lovelier—a stunning array of sparkling jewels competing with her brilliant smile.

CHAPTER 13

THAT AMANDA WASN'T the only one to notice Lady Olivia's splendor soon became evident in the sibilant wave of whispers that ensued. "Has Wrexham popped the question?" someone behind Amanda speculated. "Look at those sparklers! Surely a betrothal gift—or I'll eat my hat."

Lady Olivia and Lord Wrexham were immediately surrounded by curious friends eager to congratulate the couple, who chatted and laughed, without as much as hinting at the true state of their relationship. Lady Olivia was much celebrated, her jewels thoroughly admired. Even the haughty arbiter of fashion, Beau Brummell, lifted his eyebrow a fraction in approval.

The air suddenly filled with a universal gasp as Lord Saville made his entrance, Lurlene clinging happily to his arm, her face alight with a blinding smile. Around her throat winked an awesome double strand of diamonds, surrounding nine large square-cut sapphires of which the largest rested in the hollow of her throat. Her triumphant gaze roamed the room, inviting the compliments that must inevitably rain over her head, but the assembly stood in frozen silence.

Amanda witnessed a small petulant frown gather on Lurlene's brow, but Lord Saville looked unperturbed. Amanda could have sworn, even from the entire length of the ballroom, that a devilish smile lurked at the corners of his lips.

Lurlene's perfect face took on the wariness of a hunted animal. She gnawed on her bottom lip as she sought the reason for the peculiar tension in the room. She started violently as a male voice shouted across the room.

"I say, Saville, a dashed clever prank!"

That released the unbearable strain, and Lady Olivia, letting go of her hold on Lord Wrexham's arm, floated toward Lord Saville.

"How very naughty of you, Keith," she said in her breathy voice, but her face was bright with laughter. "I knew you were up to some trick, although I wasn't sure what."

Lurlene let out a squeal when her gaze fastened upon Lady Olivia's throat. Sapphires and diamonds, identical to her own, glittered and mocked her. Whimpering, she clapped her hands to her burning throat. Then she turned deathly pale and began to sway. Amanda feared that her stepmother was about to faint.

Balling her fists in anger, Amanda jerked to her feet. But before she could do anything, Lurlene snarled at Lord Saville, "I loathe you!" and staggered out of the room, a keening moan rising from her lips.

Amanda followed, her gaze searching for Lord Bowen, but he was nowhere in sight. The subsequent chatter rose to an outraged roar, and Amanda felt a twinge of compassion for her silly stepmama. She well deserved the lesson Lord Saville had dished out, but Amanda gave him a frosty stare as she passed him by the door. Her fingers itched to serve him a hefty wallop for insulting a member of her family— even if that member was Lurlene.

Anger churning through her, Amanda opened every door leading off the hallway until she found Lurlene in a small salon at the back. The bleak brown walls were lighted by five candles in a candelabra. Lurlene lay in a heap on the hard sofa, not caring that she creased her elegant gown. Her shoulders heaved convulsively and shattering shrieks tortured Amanda's ears as she gripped her stepmama hard, shaking her.

"Take hold of yourself, Lurlene," she ordered the hysterical woman, but Lurlene's wails rose to a crescendo. Pressing her lips together in determination, Amanda dealt her a resounding slap on the cheek. The sobs ended abruptly with a gulp, and Lurlene gazed at Amanda in shock, her eyes huge pools of despair.

"Y-you h-hit me! How dare you touch me!" Lurlene pushed Amanda savagely, making her stumble backward. Pain ripped through Amanda's chest.

"You're hysterical, Lurlene. Collect yourself," Amanda demanded, her voice muffled with pain. She watched helplessly as her stepmother grabbed one of the brocade pillows on the sofa and tore it apart, down scattering on the floor.

Lord Bowen entered just in time to behold Lurlene's rage. He slammed the door on a group of gloating onlookers and without preamble hauled his wife to her feet, pinning her arms firmly to her sides until she quieted. Then she fell limply against his chest, a torrent of tears ruining his white satin waistcoat.

"There, there, my darling," he soothed softly.

Amanda swallowed hard, trying to forgive Lurlene the

vicious shove she had dealt. Lord Bowen's eyes questioned Amanda above Lurlene's rumpled hair.

"Lord Saville played a joke on her. Lady Olivia is wearing an identical necklace—no doubt furnished by Saville," Amanda explained. As Lurlene's wails rose once more, she added, "He must have known that it's Lurlene's greatest terror to appear with a duplicate dress or jewelry."

"He's the m-most o-odious, callous man I've ever had the m-misfortune to m-meet," Lurlene sobbed. "How c-could he do this to me? I thought he cherished me."

Amanda was startled to hear Lurlene speak so lightly about her old admirer to Lord Bowen, not once thinking that her careless words might hurt him.

"I've never w-worn the *tawdry* things that other females wear, h-have I?" Lurlene straightened, her back rigid with righteousness as she demanded an answer from Lord Bowen.

"Of course not," he confirmed, patting her fondly on the head, obviously upset by the incident. He lifted his eyeglass and scrutinized the cold diamonds around his wife's neck.

"I daresay they look the real article." He rubbed his chin thoughtfully. "And Saville gave you these then?"

Lurlene stomped her dainty foot on the carpet, and with a spasmodic tug, tore the necklace from her throat. The gems shot fire as she flung them across the room just as the door opened and Lord Saville limped across the threshold. The necklace landed at his feet.

With a studied play of eyeglass he surveyed the diamonds and lifted the fiery strands with the tip of his cane. "Never cast ye pearls before swine," he muttered in an audible aside, and carelessly slipped the necklace into his pocket. Resting both hands on the top of his cane, he faced Lord Bowen and Lurlene.

Lord Bowen looked grim, his face livid with swelling

wrath. "Saville! Perhaps you can give us an explanation for this," he ordered ominously.

"A mere trinket, but I see that Lurlene doesn't approve of my gift. Was it mayhap too trifling?" Lord Saville asked blandly, his gaze landing for a moment on Amanda. The tension almost choked her, and hardly noticing it, she began to shiver.

"You gave an identical necklace to that *woman*. What is she to you—that you can insult me in such a way, publicly?" Lurlene whined, keeping a firm hold on Lord Bowen to maintain him within her power.

Lord Saville's smile was arctic. "Just like I presented you one, I gave Olivia the same in celebration of her beauty. It isn't more than fair. I swear there has been no one to hold a candle to you two since the Gunning sisters."

Lurlene hissed like a cat, her eyes narrow slits of hatred. "You gave *her* what rightfully belongs to me alone?"

Lord Saville shrugged, completely in control. "I don't see that you have monopoly on beauty, Lurlene. You're a very subjective judge, after all." His eyebrows rose in disdain. "I sincerely hoped that you'd learn something from this—perhaps mellow a bit, but I see that you're as puff-headed as ever—and always will be. You're unkind, vain, and thoroughly selfish. I swear I've never met a more egotistic person." Turning away, he aimed for the door, but Lord Bowen took two long strides to his side. Grasping Lord Saville's shoulder, he wrenched him around with a savage twist.

Fury blazing in his eyes, he slapped Lord Saville soundly on both cheeks. "You have insulted my wife; my seconds will call on yours tomorrow."

Lord Saville's eyes slitted, and his face was set into a cold mask. "Very well, if you have to make an issue of it."

Amanda expected him to leave the room then, but he had

obviously changed his mind. He stood as if rooted to the
floor, his eyes mocking Lurlene in silence until she fled to
the door, a handkerchief pressed to her eyes.

"Justin, take me home this instant!" she wailed. "I've
never been more mortified in my life, and on no occasion
will I forgive you, Keith. Not ever!"

"I hope not," he drawled with maddening calmness.

It evidently took Lord Bowen's entire willpower to
refrain from hitting Saville again before he assisted his
distraught wife outside, to bundle her off in full view of the
prying eyes of the other guests.

This night's work will be on everyone's lips tomorrow,
Amanda thought, torn between her loyalty to her father and
her instinctive approval of Lord Saville's actions—very
devious, and on the spot that hurt Lurlene the most—her
vanity. But why? The fact that he had behaved abominably
remained.

"I suppose you're planning to serve me a severe scold,
Amanda, before you flounce out of here in high dudgeon,"
he goaded, and her gaze flew to his face. His limp was more
pronounced as he slowly sauntered toward her, leaving only
a small space of charged air between them.

"Of all heartless things—" she began.

He raised a hand to stem the accusations ready to blast
from her lips. "I know! But then Lurlene deserved every bit
of it."

"You had no right." Amanda's voice was choked in
anger, but her eyes couldn't leave his face.

"I am what I choose to be. I don't make it a habit walking
around deliberately hurting people." He sounded tired, and
motioned toward the sofa. "Shall we sit down while we
argue—it tires me to stand any length of time."

"I have no intention to stay in here with *you*," Amanda
said adamantly. Since she declined to sit down, he had to

remain standing. He shifted his weight from one foot to the other, and his knuckles glared white around the silver knob of his cane.

Amanda continued, "You baffle me, milord, with your careless words, as if you have all the right in the world to insult others. At one time, in the barn outside Richmond, I began to think that a kinder character lived behind your hard face. But you've finally showed your true character to its vilest depths."

She felt hot tears of ire and disappointment crowd to her eyes, but she didn't try to remove them. She fought against her weakness, refusing to give him the upper hand.

"I would never hurt you, Amanda. You're not at all like Lurlene." On the tip of his tongue hovered the confession of his love, but he remembered Sir Digby's lovelorn face in the nick of time and clamped his lips into a thin line.

"It doesn't signify what I am—or what you think of me, Keith. For all I know, I might become an orphan soon when you meet my father in a duel, a thought more frightening than your silly opinions about me." She stared stubbornly out the pitch-black window, seeing nothing but the film of her tears. "I pray he kills you first." She didn't mean it, but the words dashed unbidden from her tongue.

To her surprise he chuckled. "That's more like it, Amanda. Bite my head off." He hauled out his snuffbox and fiddled with the lid. "However, I fail to understand how a decent man like Lord Bowen could be so foolish as to fall for Lurlene's lures."

Amanda laughed mirthlessly. "I know a score of men idolizing her, and you're no exception. I suppose the entire male side of polite society has infinitesimal brains, and is a very weak-spirited lot, to boot!"

"I understand now why you haven't married," he said virulently, stabbing his cane on the floor for emphasis. "Too full of vinegar to accept some humble gentleman, I'll be bound. I presume you'll break my uncle's heart and then laugh in his face like Lurlene did to me."

Amanda gasped and glared at him, only inches from his smoldering eyes. The air crackled between them, solid with emotions ranging from rage to undeniable attraction.

Relentlessly, he droned on, "I was right when I told Dig that you are hopelessly starchy, and that he wouldn't have to worry about you ever doing the 'wrong thing' if he married you." His voice rose. "I even went so far as to tell him that you two would suit to perfection—put each other to sleep with prosy lectures."

He doesn't yet know about Sir Digby and Pamela, Amanda thought in surprise.

"Really?" she said, her voice frigid. "Well, for your information, I told Sir Digby that you are a regular shabster—and he wholly agreed! In fact, he called you a devil's spawn," she continued in full career, bracing her fists on her hips, her eyes spewing fire. "And a blithering fool! Sir Digby is worth ten of your caliber, and a woman may consider herself fortunate to wed a kind man like him."

He drew a long sibilant breath and thrust his face within a mere inch of hers. "It's plain as pikestaff that he would make a thundering mistake getting shackled to you—and I mean to tell him that. He always listens to my advice."

"And in a pretty stew it has landed him! I should have known that you were behind Sir Digby's uncharacteristic amorous pursuits." With an afterthought, she added, "But he could do much worse than marrying me." She made as if to slip around Lord Saville, but his hand shot out with astounding speed, tangling painfully into her curls and cupping her neck with a fierce grip.

"You're not going to marry him, Amanda. Dig would never be able to handle you. He sets store by a peaceful

existence, and with you there wouldn't be much of that."
He savagely let go of her neck and she spun away with a
protest swelling in her throat. "Married to you, Dig would
stick his spoon in the wall within a year," he grated.

She gulped for air. "How dare you!" But her fire was
quenched as the door crashed open, shocking her next
stormy outburst to a sudden halt.

"Ah! *There* you are, Mandy," said the Dowager, "I've
looked for you everywhere." Her eyes filled with amazement, she stared from Amanda to Lord Saville. "Good God!
I didn't expect to find you alone with *him*, after what he's
done." She poked the door shut with her cane, then tottered
toward the sofa. Amanda would rather sink through the
floor than be the recipient of the Dowager's inevitable
lecture.

"If you're here to ring a peal over my head, you might as
well spare your breath, Lady Bowen. I assure you that
Amanda and Lord Bowen gave me a strict measure," Lord
Saville said in bored tones.

"I'm definitely not here to do the pretty. A proper set-to
it has been." She pointed an accusing gnarled finger at Lord
Saville. "You, young whippersnapper, have behaved abominably, and I have yet to find words that would adequately
convey the outrage I feel. You had no right to drag my
family through the mud. And now you have the sauce to be
closeted with my granddaughter." The Dowager's sharp
eyes drilled into Amanda.

"And you! I expected more foresight from you, miss.
We're at Almack's! If anyone witnessed your shameless
conduct you'd be finished in the eyes of polite society—and
mark my words, I won't lift a finger to help you."

Amanda had no answer. Exhaustion sapped her of all her
willpower and strength. Her mind churning, she longed for
a moment alone to collect her shattered composure. "I think

we should return home, Grandmama. Perhaps I'll be able to give you a full account of the goings-on tomorrow," she said feebly, and stumbled toward the door without looking at Lord Saville. Fortunately, the Dowager didn't pursue her analysis of his black character, but followed Amanda, her nose higher than usual.

Without reaping undue notice, Amanda and the Dowager reached the street. The other guests had returned to the ballroom to gossip and to partake of refreshments. Sir Digby and Pamela stood waiting on the steps outside, and Sir Digby assisted the ladies inside their carriage before calling for his own.

"I don't know what to say," he muttered, his face red with embarrassment. "My nephew is a deuced hothead."

The Dowager patted his arm with unusual kindness. "Don't worry your head over it. Besides, you can't help that you're related to him," she said with a cackle. In stentorian tones she ordered the coachman to drive them home, and Sir Digby was left behind, his face blurred with confusion as he waved weakly.

Amanda shrank into the merciful darkness of the coach, hoping that the Dowager was too tired to continue the topic of the dastardly Lord Saville. But her hopes were soon squashed.

"I cannot believe the *gall* of that man!" the Dowager began, her eyes bearing down on Amanda.

Pamela came to Amanda's assistance, not knowing everything that had transpired behind the closed door of the salon at Almack's. "I daresay Lord Saville acted very ungentlemanly, but as to what I heard whispered afterward, the other guests cheered for him—in fact praised him for his audacity. No one has ever dared to put Lurlene in her place before."

"I agree that she sorely needed a lesson, and we don't

know what prompted Saville to act in such a manner, some old quarrel most likely. Nevertheless, he acted ungentlemanly, and I will not stand for it. And Justin is too mealy-mouthed to do something about it."

The information about the challenge hovered on Amanda's lips, but she held it back, not wanting to cause the Dowager further worry.

Pamela tried to maneuver the talk away from Lord Saville. "Lady Olivia Lexington thought it was famous fun. It didn't bother her that Lurlene received an identical necklace."

The Dowager snorted. "But Livvy is a very amiable character—not at all like Lurlene. And she can take a good joke, especially when receiving such a handsome gift."

"You thought it was a good joke then?" Amanda probed gently.

The Dowager's whoops of mirth filled the interior of the carriage. "Of course I did, you peagoose. Haven't had so much fun since Lady Ashborough, Saville's grandmother, danced on the tables at the Duchess of Chandos's ball fifty years ago." She seemed to gather her thoughts, wiping a tear of glee from her eye. "I'm burning to know what prompted Saville to behave so outrageously. Lurlene must have goaded him beyond endurance." She gave an ostrich feather tickling her brow a violent tug, causing the turban to tilt at a rakish angle above her right eye. "His big show of affection toward Lurlene was nothing but a big hoax. Wily as a fox, Saville is." The Dowager quieted abruptly, evidently thinking hard. "I simply have to find out what Lurlene did to him."

Amanda was grateful that the Dowager's thoughts were diverted from herself, but she knew that the discussion wasn't yet over.

She got a reprieve, because upon returning to South

Street, lights glowed in the best cream and gold salon. Ensconced in the most comfortable chair in front of a small fire sat Lady Elfina Waring, her bony shoulders encased in a black cashmere shawl, and her dark eyes haughtily regarding the baffled ladies before her.

"There you are! I thought you'd keep me waiting all night," she said in her oddly pinched and nasal voice.

CHAPTER 14

LADY PAMELA RUSHED forward to embrace her grandmother with obvious delight, but like the Dowager, Lady Elfina had limited patience with outbursts of emotion.

"Out at all hours of the night," she grumbled, leveling a disapproving gaze at her granddaughter, but Pamela paid little heed to Lady Waring's displeasure.

"I'm having a glorious time, Grandmother. So many things to see, and I've made so many new friends."

Lady Waring rose, a tall gaunt figure giving the impression of a ruffled crow in her black gown and voluminous woolen shawl. The old face was hollow and pale, but the black stare was alive and icy as it bore down on the Dowager.

"It's clear that Ambrosia is leading you right into the very depths of vice, Pamela. I see that I've arrived in the nick of time."

Lady Pamela's eyes went blank with surprise. "What do you mean? I'm having the best time of my life."

"I don't doubt that," Lady Waring said with heavy

sarcasm and sniffed. "Well? Are you going to stand in that doorway all night, Ambrosia, gaping?"

The Dowager found her usual aplomb, and for one moment forgetting her stiff knee joints she sailed forth regally, to seat herself opposite Lady Waring. Amanda followed suit in a more subdued manner. She was exhausted, and whatever sermon about the evils of vice Lady Waring was about to deliver could only push her deeper into despondency.

"Elfina, what has brought you to London without as much as a messenger informing us of your arrival?" the Dowager asked.

Lady Waring snorted. "*You* should know that, Ambrosia. It's all because of the letter you sent me. I had to come immediately to save my lamb from the clutches of that—that *upstart*!"

"Who are you referring to, Grandmother?" Pamela asked in baffled tones. She exchanged uneasy glances with Amanda.

"That Knottiswood person, of course. Ambrosia told me he has proposed, and I also received a long-winded letter from him a few days ago, where he voiced his intentions to wed you just as soon as it could be arranged. But I might as well tell you right now, Pamela, you can't have him! I won't sit quietly by and watch my nearest kin make an unsuitable match."

The Dowager made a noise of outrage, and she appeared to grow several inches as she stared at her much taller sister through her eyeglass.

"That is a bag of moonshine, and well you know it, Elfina! Sir Digby is a splendid match. Pamela will be happy with him, and he will treat her with consideration and all the comforts befitting her rank."

"Fudge!" Lady Elfina brandished a very long finger

under the Dowager's nose. "Sir Digby Knottiswood is connected to *trade*, and you of all persons should know that. But in view of your age, I suppose your memory has dimmed. I will not tolerate to have our pedigree tainted with that man's blood."

Nothing could get the Dowager's hackles up more speedily than the mentioning of her age, especially by a sister ten years her junior.

Her voice frosty, and her color high, she sputtered, "Hoity-toity! Sir Digby's relatives are nothing if not well-born. Why, he can count marquesses and dukes among his relations. And if you rushed over here to speak to me of Sir Digby's connections, you're the one who is tottering on the brink of dotage."

"Really? Well, let me stir the murky depths of your memory. Sir Digby's grandmother was *trade*. Knottis-wood's grandfather married her for her wealth, all acquired from her father's vast coaching business."

The Dowager laughed mirthlessly. "It's ancient history, Elfina. Besides, if you dared to take a closer look at our family tree, you'd know we claim kinship to trade. Well—a very long time ago, of course."

Lady Waring seemed to shrink, and Amanda took a deep breath. "Perhaps we should discuss this further in the morning. We're exhausted and view everything darker than it really is," she said tentatively.

"Tomorrow I will take Pamela back to the country. I knew it was a mistake to let her come here. London is nothing if not filled with temptations to lure young females from the path of innocence."

Amanda was aware of the unease gradually filling Pamela beside her on the sofa, and she squeezed her friend's cold hand comfortingly. Amanda had an uneasy premonition the difficulties were only just beginning, and she sighed.

"I'll refuse to go with her," Pamela whispered agitatedly into Amanda's ear.

"Of course. I'm sure Grandmama will handle her," Amanda said *sotto voce*.

Pamela looked dubious, and Amanda felt a twinge of doubt herself as she looked at the two old sisters measuring each other up like two cocks in a cockfight.

She stood resolutely, pulling Pamela with her.

"Grandmama, we're excessively tired, and I beg your permission to retire."

"Yes, of course. I will see to it that Elfina is comfortably settled," the Dowager said absentmindedly, and waved them off with an impatient hand.

Pamela made a movement forward to kiss her grandmother, but Amanda gave her a tug and shoved her out the door. They refrained from speaking until they were safely inside Pamela's room. Amanda pushed her cousin down on the bed, and held both her hands on Pamela's shoulders to calm her. "There is only one thing to do. You have to pay Digby a visit the first thing tomorrow morning. Together you'll have to convince Great-aunt Elfina that you love each other, and that you won't let her interfere. Then she'll have to give you her blessing."

Lady Pamela nodded miserably, her eyes huge with worry, and Amanda suspected that her friend didn't have faith in her words, but Amanda was too tired to argue. "Chin up! You cannot let your grandmother ruin your happiness."

They embraced and bid each other goodnight. Amanda left Pamela and entered the haven of her own bedroom next door. Meg sat nodding in a chair in front of the open window, oblivious to the humid gusts of wind whipping through the curtains. Amanda sent her to bed with the assurance that she could perfectly well undress herself.

The heavy air smelled of imminent rain, and a low brooding rumble in the distance promised that the approaching storm would be a violent one. Amanda contemplated shutting the window, but she could not stand the closed-in atmosphere. The storm matched the turmoil of her mind, and her movements were leaden as she undressed. A headache was beginning to throb at the base of her neck.

Perspiration glued her hair to her temples as the storm moved closer. The air had turned breathless and hot. Amanda tossed in her bed, the covers a tangle at her feet. On the inside of her eyelids, feverish images leaped and danced. Keith's face taunted her, his bold lips claiming hers in a ravishing kiss. Her father's hurt and angry face swam before her. She saw him soaked in blood on the misty ground of a clearing surrounded by tall elms. Then the prone figure turned into Lord Saville, his face pale in death. She whimpered and sat bolt upright as the first lightning slashed the pitch darkness. Thunder crashed above and she automatically slapped her palms to her ears. Another lightning glared, slicing through her agonized thoughts. The two men she loved were going to fight each other—perhaps to death. Duels were illegal, and Amanda knew that if a gentleman killed his opponent, he had to flee the country and never return. Waves of apprehension churned through her, mingling with a sense of hopelessness. Was one of them going to die in a pool of blood? Whatever the outcome of the duel, it was sure to bring her heartache. She had to do something to stop it.

Sleep eluded Lord Saville as well. Listening to the thunder, he limped like a wraith from room to room in the Saville mansion on Grosvenor Square. The luxuriously decorated salons and his treasured *objets d' art* failed to give him any consolation as he concentrated wholeheartedly on the problems in his mind. If the evening had ended as planned, he would have lain in peaceful sleep by now, content with his revenge upon Lurlene. How could he have known she would resort to hysterics in public? She should have accepted his joke graciously and learned her lesson— that she wasn't the center of the universe. A new life should have stretched before him, but instead he was haunted by guilt. The memory of Amanda's accusing black gaze taunted him as soon as he closed his eyes.

He shuddered and sipped some claret from the glass in his hand to wash away the sour taste of failure in his mouth. He had discovered that it was no business of his trying to change Lurlene. He would never get the smallest of apologies from her.

His lips quirked bitterly. Drawing aside the gold brocade curtain in the long gold and blue drawing room, he gazed at the dark turbulent skies. Bluish jagged light illuminated the trees in the square and outlined the buildings on the opposite side.

Besides the memory of Amanda's dark accusing eyes, he would remember the violent storm on this dreadful night. And he would have to learn to live with the grueling pain in his leg for the rest of his life.

He flung himself into a chair as desolation seeped through him and a muscle worked in his jaw. He knew he would get no peace until he had spoken with Amanda again. But first he would have to meet Lord Bowen at Barn Elms.

Early the next morning, long before the hour when the *beau monde* usually stirred, Amanda was dressed and ready to go out. She could not swallow one morsel of toast, and she choked down her tea in a hurry. Longing to relieve the tension within her, she needed to get to her father's house without delay. She would have to make her father see reason and not fight Keith. The marquess was known as an excellent shot and swordsman.

Lord Bowen was waiting to be shaved by his valet as Lipton, the butler, knocked and entered his master's bedchamber. "Miss Amanda is here to see you, milord. Says 'tis urgent."

Lord Bowen slanted a glance toward the door. "Show her in."

Amanda rushed into her father's bedroom, her cheeks red with exertion as she had run all the way from South Street to Berkley Square.

"What's the matter, m'dear?" Lord Bowen asked kindly, and pulled off the sheet covering the front of his shirt. "Is it Mother?" He motioned to his valet to leave the room, and Amanda waited until they were alone. She shot a glance at the door leading to Lurlene's bedchamber, but not a sound emanated from there.

"No, Grandmama is fine. I'm here to warn you not to fight, Father." Amanda's voice broke and she covered her face with her hands. "Lord Saville doesn't have any scruples. He'll kill you, I'm sure of it."

"There, there. Don't take on so." Lord Bowen placed his arms around her and patted her head as he used to do when she was a child.

"I beg of you not to fight—" Her voice faded in a sob.

Lord Bowen sighed and handed her a handkerchief. "The code of honor cannot be broken, dearest. Besides, I cannot stand by and watch Saville insult my wife without issuing some kind of retribution."

"Grandmama thinks Lurlene has done something awful to Lord Saville," she whispered.

Lord Bowen looked older, deep lines slashing from

nostrils to lips. "Perhaps. According to the gossip, he was supposed to marry her last year, but she jilted him. I have never found out the reason." He smiled blandly. "It's not the kind of subject one discusses with Lurlene, y'know. It's bound to set off her hysterics."

"Lurlene can switch them on and off," Amanda said uncharitably. She regretted her words instantly when her father's face stiffened with sadness. "I'm sorry," she murmured.

"I know you never saw eye to eye with Lurlene, sweetings, but I had hoped you might learn to get along."

Probably never, Amanda thought sadly. "I'll try. Just give me some more time to get used to her."

"If you had your own family, it might be different. You would understand our—er, attraction."

Amanda remembered Lord Saville's smoky green eyes, the touch of his strong fingers, and his bold lips that had the power to melt her reason. "Yes—you're probably right." She turned away so that her father could not see the embarrassment tingeing her cheeks. "I have come in vain, haven't I?"

Lord Bowen lifted his shoulders apologetically. "I cannot stop the duel."

Amanda ran out of the room, too distraught to think coherently. She had one more chance to stop the confrontation. However much she balked at the idea, she would visit Lord Saville and plead with him. Her heart made a wild lurch in her chest at the thought of facing him. She pictured herself on the granite steps of his mansion in Grosvenor Square, his butler giving her a disapproving stare.

Unchaperoned young ladies did not visit gentlemen at any time. But what did such trifles matter when her father's life was at stake?

At Hill Street she hailed a hackney cab and ordered the driver to take her the few blocks to Grosvenor Square. Her palms were wet with nervousness, and she tapped her foot on the dingy straw-covered floor.

The quiet spaciousness and elegance of the square made her courage ebb. The hack stopped with a jolt outside Lord Saville's imposing front door, and Amanda swallowed hard to ease the parched feeling of her throat as she pressed a coin into the grimy hand of the driver. Then she took a few leaden steps toward the entrance. Two stone lions guarded the stairs, toothy gaps widened in eternal roars. The tall windows on both sides of the door looked unseeing upon the square; the heavy curtains were drawn.

Amanda heaved a sigh of disappointment when she noticed that the brass knocker was gone. Saville was not in residence. She rapped on the door, expecting some servant to open it and tell her where the marquess had gone. But no one moved within. The house held a brooding, empty silence. Finally she slipped down the steps, not daring to linger. Where could he be? Oh, dear God, how would she live through the next twenty-four hours?

That evening, after an intolerable day of listening to the Dowagers' grating arguments, she retired to her bedroom to write a note to Lord Saville. Her hands trembled so much she could barely form the words:

Lord Saville,

I beg of you to reconsider your duel with my father. It is not fair that you would desire to kill he who has never done anything to hurt you. Besides, duels are illegal. Has it never occurred to you the heartbreak my father's death would cause my family? If you had any decency, you would apologize to my stepmother for your atrocious behavior, or at least tell me the reason for it so that I could apologize for you.

Amanda scanned the note, dissatisfied, but there was no time left for reformulating her request.

His answer arrived with the footman she had sent to the Saville mansion carrying her note:

Dear Miss Bowen,
   I cannot comply with your request. To find the answer you're seeking, you should ask your stepmother.

                                        Y'r most obedient servant,
                                        Saville

Amanda crumpled the note and sank down on the sofa in the green salon. What had she expected? An apologetic letter in which he asked for her help? Anger burned through her, and she hurled the note across the room. She would get no answer since Lurlene was confined to her bedroom, refusing to see anyone but Lord Bowen. There was nothing Amanda could do but await the grim dawn.

The next morning, thirty-six hours after the uproar at Almack's, Lord Saville met Lord Bowen at Barn Elms, a dueling spot well hidden from the suspicious eye of the law. The scent of damp earth floated from the ground. Morning mist swirled around the duelers' topboots as they trod among the tussocks, and the leaves hung heavy with dew above their heads. Dawn was no more than a bluish pink haze in the east.

Sir Anthony Fanshawe had reluctantly agreed to act as Lord Saville's second. The marquess had summoned Sir Digby with a note on the previous evening, but the message had remained unanswered. Lord Bowen was seconded by an old friend.

Lord Saville limped more heavily than usual, and the excruciating pain in his leg forced perspiration to his face and made his stomach churn with nausea. His features pale and set, he faced Lord Bowen.

Lord Bowen looked older and quite unhappy.

"You still want to go through with the duel?" Saville asked flatly.

"I'm a peace-loving man," Lord Bowen said tiredly, "but the honor of my family is at stake. You shall pay for your insult, Saville." He stared narrowly at the younger man. "I knew you always were a hothead, but insulting women in public is quite beyond the pale. I never imagined you would stoop that low."

"There are a lot of things you don't know, Bowen," Saville murmured with a cold smile. "Shall we get to it? I have a breakfast engagement later."

Amanda's father laughed hollowly. "Yes—but you won't be able to attend." On that hostile note they moved to the opposite sides of the clearing.

Sir Anthony minced through the tall wet grass with the flat black case of dueling pistols under his arm.

"Of all ridiculous things, this takes the prize," muttered Sir Anthony to Lord Bowen's second, his voice dripping with displeasure as he inspected the sleek Manton pistols on their black velvet pad. "If the authorities get wind of this—"

"Make haste," the second broke in, his gaze darting uneasily among the trees. "It should be over in a few minutes, and the law none the wiser—unless one of the duelists dies. . . ."

Grim-faced, the two seconds loaded and primed the pistols while Saville and Bowen went through the ritual of taking off their hats, coats and waistcoats. A gust of wind shook dew from the leaves, splattering their heads with a cascade of drops and fluttering their white shirt sleeves. Mist clung chilly and insinuating to their legs. Calmly Lord Saville placed his garments in his black, covered carriage and accepted the primed pistol from Sir Anthony. It lay cold and deadly in his hand, the hair-trigger ready to go off at the slightest pressure. Lord Saville turned his back to Lord Bowen, the older man's unyielding shoulders butting hard against his own. The sound of Sir Anthony's voice echoed ghostly in his ears. Perspiration trickled down his spine, gluing the shirt to his back. The pain impulses from his leg seemed to fill his entire brain.

"One . . . two . . . three . . ."

Lord Saville automatically measured the twelve steps, turned, aimed, and fired high above Lord Bowen's head. The deafening cracks split the morning peace apart, and a white-hot spear ripped into Saville's leg. With a shout, he dropped his pistol to the ground and crumpled.

From the interior of Lord Bowen's carriage emerged a surgeon, bribed to stand by just in case blood was let.

Saville cursed roundly, every nerve-ending fighting the torture in his leg. Lord Bowen hurried to his side, face creased with worry.

"I swear I didn't mean to hit you; I aimed way to the right," Bowen vowed, gripping Lord Saville's shoulder, eager to make amends.

Through the veils of his pain, the marquess shot him an annoyed, incredulous look. "Are you blind as a bat? This is my leg, dammit!"

The surgeon pried loose Saville's fingers clamped over the wound, but the marquess pushed him away. His black pantaloons was stained darker with blood, and the fabric hung in tattered ribbons where the ball had crashed through his leg.

The surgeon gingerly touched the pool of blood under Lord Saville's leg. "Looks like a clean shot; the ball exited on the other side. I will have to bind it tightly to stop the flow," he announced and unceremoniously made Lord Saville lie down on the wet grass. He ordered Lord Bowen, standing crestfallen nearby, to fetch brandy, but when Lord Bowen returned with the flask, the marquess had struggled to his feet and was staggering toward his carriage. His leg dragged awkwardly behind him.

"Wait!" called Lord Bowen, hurrying after the younger man.

Lord Saville swore viciously as Bowen touched his arm. He veered off to the side, his face twisted in pain. "Leave me alone," he grated between stiff lips.

"You cannot go like this. Let the surgeon at least bind your wound."

Saville snarled and hoisted himself into his carriage. He howled in pain as his injured leg slid along the step. Hauling it inside, he slammed the door behind him and the horses leaped forward, jolting the wheels out of the mud.

Lord Bowen ran after it, brandishing the flask, but the carriage disappeared around the bend in the lane. Lord Bowen had his own riding horse bound to the back of his coach, which he had brought just in case he'd be wounded. He unleashed the reins and jumped into the saddle. "I'll go after him," he yelled at the surgeon and the seconds.

"No!" called Sir Anthony. "There is no way of knowing what he might do in that wild state."

But Lord Bowen wasn't listening. "Be careful," Sir Anthony called after him. The seconds looked at each other uneasily, shaking their heads.

Amanda's father spied Lord Saville's carriage pulled up

outside an inn. The coachman was standing in the yard, scratching his head.

"Milord 'as fallen in a dead faint," he said, his old forehead creased in worry as Lord Bowen alighted. "What shall I do wiw 'im?"

Bowen glanced inside the carriage. The marquess was sprawled across the seat, deathly pale, and his leg twisting at a sharp angle from his knee. Blood trickled steadily from the wound.

"We have to find a surgeon posthaste." He thought for a moment. "We'll take him to South Street. 'Tis the closest address. Besides, my mother's abigail is an excellent nurse."

"Aye, then I'll fetch milord's doctor, th' one who 'as been treatin' milord's leg afore."

Half an hour later, the carriage pulled up outside the Dowager's house. Lord Saville had recovered from his swoon and was trying to sit up.

The two men silently measured each other for a long moment, and then Lord Bowen offered his hand, helping the younger man outside. As Billings appeared, Bowen ordered him to send a footman around to Doctor Kingsley, Lord Saville's physician.

"Where are we?" the wounded marquess enquired, his voice barely a croak.

"At the Dowager Bowen's house."

Lord Saville protested, but he was slowly sliding back into unconsciousness. The coachman and one of the footmen carried him inside.

Amanda flew down the stairs, her face as white as a sheet. "Is he dead?"

Lord Bowen cradled his daughter close. "No, m'dear, but he's wounded in the leg. My aim was terrible! Couldn't see very well at that distance, I'm afraid. All a blur, and I shot him. I didn't intend to, y'know," he added as he saw the outrage on Amanda's face.

"You could have killed him," she breathed, her eyes flashing fire.

"Yes, I know. But he'll be fine after the surgeon sees to him. I'll go up now and give him some brandy to ease the pain while waiting for the physician to arrive."

Amanda wished she could have accompanied her father to the yellow guestroom where the servants had settled Lord Saville, but propriety forbade her to enter.

Wringing her hands, she paced the corridor outside the room, wondering what was transpiring between her father and Lord Saville. When Doctor Kingsley arrived half an hour later and stepped into the room, she caught a glimpse of the marquess's strained pale face against the pillows.

Dear God, let him get well, she prayed, her heart aching with misery.

CHAPTER 15

THE BRANDY, coupled with the blade-sharp pain in his leg, made the marquess nauseated and dizzy. In his need to vent his agony, he laughed wildly. His tormentor Lord Bowen's worried face wavered above him. He closed his eyes, hoping the vision would disappear, but when he opened them again Lord Bowen was still there. He lifted his leaden arm to take a swipe at the man, but somehow the image flickered and faded.

Lord Saville laughed until tears stood in his eyes. More pain ripped through him, and he gripped the bedcovers convulsively. Someone jerked his tortured leg. "Damn your eyes!" he swore, and fainted.

When he came to, it was like swimming in a murky pond with his eyes open. Black specks and brown foggy swirls danced in his vision. His body felt numb and cold, and a dull ache pounded in his leg. But it was less painful than it had been . . . when? What time was it? How long had he been lying in this strange bed? Lord Bowen's face hovered above him again. Saville blinked twice to focus on the pale features. The face materialized out of a dimness that stemmed from the drawn curtains in the room. He suddenly remembered the duel, remembered everything, and a deep sadness spread in his chest.

"Your honor is intact, Lord Bowen," he gasped. "I suppose I earned this." He pointed toward his leg.

Lord Bowen shrugged and looked embarrassed. "This whole business is pure folly." He squinted toward the plaster ceiling. "What would you say to a bit of breakfast, old boy?"

"I could use some more brandy," the marquess ground out between clenched teeth as an especially vicious pain stabbed his leg.

Birds seemed to twitter in his head, but it was the maid's voice surely? Did he hear the name Amanda?

Lord Bowen's grip brought him out of the undulating mists of his dreams. The older man's arm around his shoulders was strong, dragging him up in bed. The butler was there, plumping up the pillows.

As his dizziness faded, Lord Saville said, "We need to talk, and then I'll be on my way home. Can't impose on you any longer." Was that weak voice really his? He was too tired to protest as Lord Bowen placed the tray over his legs and draped a huge napkin over his borrowed nightshirt.

"Breakfast first, old chap."

Lord Saville surveyed the tray. Steam curled from the hot tea, and the buttered toast made him feel sick. With dismay he noticed how much his hand shook as he lifted the teacup. As he swallowed the brew he happened to look up, and was surprised to see another vision—a lovely one. From behind Lord Bowen's broad back stepped Amanda, beautiful in a buttercup yellow gown. She looked so pale and drawn.

Instinctively, he reached out to her. Her lovely lips trembled as she held his tired hand in her cool grip. Her touch was so soothing, a balm for his agony. Her strength seemed to seep up his arm.

"I've come to feed you," she said. "Grandmama tried to stop me, but I-I *had* to see you." She stood so close he could smell the flowery scent of her perfume. It reminded him of a warm lazy summer day. He wanted to close his arms around her.

"I'm glad you insisted." He swallowed as she held the teacup to his lips. The strong sweet tea warmed his stomach, and he felt better.

"I wanted to thank you for not killing my father," she whispered in his ear. "I'm sorry he shot you." She spooned something warm and cinnamon-flavored between his lips. "Porridge," she explained. "Grandmama insisted it's the best cure for every ailment."

Swallowing automatically, he stared at her. She was beautiful, her skin so soft and inviting. He wanted to tell her how comforting her presence was. Somehow he managed to form his thoughts into words. "You're the best cure any man could have at hand," he ground out, noticing how her cheeks reddened.

"You shouldn't speak," she said, giving him more tea.

Lord Bowen's voice rumbled in the background and the door opened and closed. Then he stood at Amanda's side by the bed.

Lord Saville sagged against the pillows, closing his eyes and clamping his teeth against the pain pulsing fire through his leg.

The base of a glass grated against the wooden surface of the tray. "Here, drink this brandy, Keith, you'll feel better for it," Amanda's father said.

Lord Saville reached blindly for the glass, and took a hearty swig. The liquid spread warmth, relief to his tormented nerves. "Thank you," he murmured huskily, and straightened. "Ahh." He managed to focus on Lord Bowen, forcing himself to ignore Amanda's presence for the moment.

A hint of amusement gleamed in the other man's eyes. "I guess I owe you an apology for winging you," Lord Bowen said wryly.

Lord Saville held up a restraining hand. "No, I surely owe *you* one." He lifted his glass with jerky movements and downed the rest of the brandy in one gulp.

Lord Bowen shrugged. "I'm well aware of your old attachment to Lurlene."

Saville laughed harshly. "That is Fate's cruel joke." He hesitated. How could he tell Lord Bowen the truth? "Perhaps I should speak with you alone," he said with a sideways glance at Amanda.

Lord Bowen placed his arm around her shoulders. "Why? She's been very worried and has a right to hear whatever we have to discuss, I think." Lord Bowen studied his daughter's face closely. "Are you prepared to listen?"

She nodded. Her eyes were darker than usual and filled with questions.

Lord Saville sighed. "I find that I have erred. It was wrong to embarrass Lurlene in public."

Lord Bowen nodded his understanding. "Yes, bitterness can eat a man alive. I take it your bitterness stems from Lurlene jilting you." When Lord Saville remained silent, Lord Bowen chuckled. "I don't know if I should say this, but I thought the joke with the necklace was well-played. In your shoes I might have done the same thing, you know." He sighed deeply. "Lurlene is a handful at best, and much good it does her to see that not all the world is prostrated at her feet. And she'll have to learn that fashions and fal-lals are not the hub of the universe."

A look of utter amazement crept into Lord Saville's eyes

at Bowen's cheerful words. Never had he imagined that
Amanda's father would take this view. Greatly relieved, and
with brandy fumes lying like cotton in his veins, he could
relax against the pillows. "I'm glad you don't harbor any
grudge against me."

"I don't." Lord Bowen threw his head back and laughed.
"I'm sorry," he managed to choke out, "but you might have
been wed to her if it weren't for Olivia Lexington."

Saville's smoky green eyes never left Lord Bowen's face,
knowing at last that he would know the truth behind
Lurlene's sudden marriage to Lord Bowen.

Lord Bowen pushed a hand through his hair and walked
around to the other side of the bed. "Lady Olivia Lexington
made no secret about being attracted to me." He took a deep
breath. "At my age, it's very flattering to have a young
woman casting sheep's eyes. I was easily taken in. As you
know, Olivia has an abundance of charm. I almost came to
the point of proposing to her." His lips curled into a wry
smile. "Then Lurlene began to flutter her eyelashes at me,
I'm afraid my vanity grew rather large with the two loveliest
young females in London flirting with me. You might find
this unbelievable, but I fell in love with Lurlene. I know she
can't hold a candle to Olivia's charm, but there is something
so helpless, so endearing about Lurlene. My protective
instincts were raised, and I'm convinced that she loves me
in return. However, it will take a long time before she learns
not to always put herself first. Perhaps your lesson was the
first step in the right direction, and—er, the child she's
expecting will surely help." Lord Bowen sounded drained,
but he gazed benevolently at Saville. "Can you forgive her
for jilting you?"

Lord Saville's lips quirked. "I never loved Lurlene."

Lord Bowen's face fell in surprise. "If you didn't care,
why the revenge?"

The pain in his leg had haunted Saville for a year, but he could not mention it. "Well, I thought my revenge would clear the air, but I don't feel the relief I expected. Revenge never does any good." He clamped his lips shut, and a long silence stretched between them. A bird trilled outside the window and eased the tension.

"Keith, that is an evasive answer if I ever heard one." Lord Bowen waited, but Lord Saville averted his face. "Well, I cannot force you to tell me the truth."

Lord Bowen cleared his throat and gave Amanda a worried glance. "I'll never understand why Lurlene and Olivia were fighting about me. Why me? Why not some well-heeled young gentleman?" He pointed at Lord Saville. "Like him. I daresay it was Lurlene's idea. When she found out that Olivia was interested in me, she wanted to best her—always best her."

Lord Saville's gaze rushed to Lord Bowen's face. "And she did! But why does she maintain a grudge toward Olivia Lexington?"

Lord Bowen laughed dryly. "Livvy didn't seem heartbroken when losing me. Lurlene's goal was to make her rival miserable, and when she failed, she began to hate Olivia. She could never stand Olivia's charm." He shot a quick glance at Lord Saville. "I'm painting Lurlene very heartless, but I know her true feelings. She found that she really cared about me—something of a miracle, considering that she's so—childish."

"Yes, but she should count herself extremely fortunate to get you, Lord Bowen. I would never have had the patience to stand her tantrums." Lord Saville let out a laugh which jarred his leg. "I guess I should thank you for taking her off my hands."

Lord Bowen joined in the merriment and poured more brandy in the marquess's glass.

"Men," Amanda muttered.

The marquess watched her slender form as she began to pace the floor. Something warm floated through him, and his throat clogged. When she came to stand over him, he dodged her accusing gaze.

"Grandmama said there must be something—serious underlying your cruel joke," Amanda commented. "Why do you evade the explanation?"

Lord Saville realized that although the question was put before him that bluntly, he could not tattle on Lurlene. If he avenged himself a hundred times, he would never be able to transfer the pain in his leg to the person who was responsible for it—Lurlene. "I'm very tired now," he said, averting his eyes. He was exhausted, and as soon as he closed his eyes, he began to drift. He heard Amanda's voice from very far away.

"I'll fetch Lurlene," she said, heatedly. "And find out the truth if 'tis the last thing I do." *No*, cried a voice in his head, and he wanted to stop her, but no words formed on his lips.

Keith heard Lord Bowen speak, but could not decipher his words. He sounded angry and agitated. Keith berated himself; why had he ever instigated the blasted revenge? That was the last thought in his head before he slid into darkness.

When he awakened next, the curtains were open and light flowed warm and golden through the windows. The room was cheerful, as if the sunlight had been plastered right into the walls with the paint. The furniture was graceful Queen Anne style and the sofas were covered with flower-embroidered pillows. A landscape graced one of the walls. It looked like a Gainsborough, but he could not see it very clearly.

A movement at the end of the bed captured his attention.

It was Doctor Kingsley, and beside him stood Lord Bowen and Amanda. His heart leaped at the sight of her. He wanted to speak with her, to reveal his feelings, but what could he say?

"Ah! Young man, already awake, eh?" boomed the white-haired and bespectacled doctor. "I had hoped I could examine your leg before you woke up." He removed the covers from the leg. "I have good news for you, milord. The shot hit you clean through the old break in the leg, and I've been able to set it right this time." He patted the wooden splints bracing the leg. "I'll be as bold as to say that your old pain might leave you at last. Once this is healed, you'll be as right as a trivet, y' know."

Saville thought there was something wrong with his ears. The leg ached, but it was less painful than it had been before the shot. It was as if an old nagging worry had left him and there was peace at last. He dared not speak for fear that his voice would fail him. He only nodded, hoping that his eyes conveyed his gratitude. Fate had some strange twists, he mused. "I should return home. Don't want to be a burden."

"You're not a burden, and we have some unfinished business," said Lord Bowen, and ushered the doctor to the door.

Lord Saville waited with apprehension. Amanda looked so forbidding; he wondered if it was hatred or worry clouding her eyes. He winced as he heard Lurlene's peevish voice.

"I have no desire to visit Keith in his bedroom," she complained, but nonetheless she advanced across the yellow and light-blue carpet to stand beside the bed. Her eyes were both contemptuous and frightened as she looked down on him. "What do you want with me, Keith?" she asked icily.

"Nothing," he said between stiff lips, wishing she would remove her presence. "I didn't send for you."

"*I* wanted you here," said Amanda. "You have something to tell us, don't you, Lurlene, something concerning the day you jilted Lord Saville."

Lurlene pinched her lips together in anger. "I don't have to explain anything to you."

Lord Bowen placed his arm around her and held her tightly. "I think you haven't been quite fair to Lord Saville. I promise I won't be angry at you, whatever happened that day."

She glanced at the marquess with narrowed eyes. "I have no idea what lies he has told you, but one fact is clear: I could never have stopped that stupid horse from kicking him."

"Horse?" Lord Bowen pulled his eyebrows together.

"Yes . . . the one supposed to pull old Admiral Riverwood from the stream." She glanced uneasily from Lord Bowen to Amanda. "Keith hasn't told you?"

"No," Bowen said. "You'd better start from the beginning."

"And don't lie," Amanda admonished.

Lord Saville looked at her, wanting to squeeze her hand, to reassure her. He prayed Lurlene would tell the whole truth. It was hardly likely. "Tell them why we got betrothed, Lurlene. Please," he begged.

"Oh, very well." Lurlene plopped herself without ado on the edge of the bed. "I had a bet with Lady Olivia that I could get Keith to propose to me within a fortnight." She glanced uneasily at Lord Bowen. "It was only a lark. Keith has never offered for any lady, so we thought it might be a good joke to find out if we could engage his interest."

"I see," said Lord Bowen, rubbing his chin. He had paled considerably. "And did you succeed?"

Lurlene shot Keith a venomous glance. "No, well, yes! He proposed to me . . . but only after I had asked him to have my carriage mended. I stayed at Ashborough Castle overnight—unchaperoned." She sighed.

Lord Bowen laughed, easing the tension in the room. "Carriage? What *really* happened?"

Lurlene's head wilted on her slender neck, her shoulders slumping. "I won the bet, 'cause Olivia never got Keith to do anything." She knotted her fist and pounded the marquess in the shoulder, until Lord Bowen pulled her away. "Stupid, silly, Keith!"

"You *forced* him to propose?" Amanda sounded incredulous, and her knuckles shone white around the bedpost.

Lord Bowen looked at Keith, seeking confirmation. He nodded. "I had no intention of marrying Lurlene, but after she spent the night at Ashborough, I was honor-bound to offer for her. One of the shackles of her carriage had broken and the horse was gone, right outside the gates to the estate."

Lurlene pouted. "You make it sound so *devious*. We've always been neighbors, after all. My groom went to speak with your stable-master about mending the carriage. When he returned, I had already, well, sought shelter inside the mansion." She tittered uncomfortably.

"I had a great surprise waiting for me at the breakfast table the next morning," Lord Saville said ruefully. "I don't know who you managed to bribe to tamper with your carriage—and why you traveled unchaperoned—but I knew you had trapped me."

"I thought you really liked me, until the night of that dreadful necklace," Lurlene said angrily. She clung to Sir Justin. "I'm glad you shot him in the leg."

"So why did you jilt Lord Saville, Lurlene?" Amanda prodded inexorably.

Silence fell heavy in the room.

"Well?" Lord Bowen urged.

Embarrassment flamed on Lurlene's cheeks. "A week after our betrothal, we had been to a gathering at a neighboring estate. The weather was terrible, and I was afraid I would catch inflammation of the lungs since my slippers were soaked through." She sighed. "That stupid Admiral Riverwood's carriage had broken the bridge across a stream. One of the horses was dead and the other stood beside the water. The carriage was tilting halfway into the stream. Keith tried to lift the old man out, but the water was too deep." Her voice became a whine. "I was so cold and wet, and decided to ride the horse home. Keith could easily assist the admiral by himself."

"You know I could not do that," said Keith, his voice tight with anger. "I needed that horse to help me pull the admiral out."

"I needed the horse more," Lurlene spat, stomping her foot. "When Keith tried to stop me, the horse reared and kicked him in the shin. Well, you both know that he has had a limp."

Agitated, Keith leaned halfway out of the bed, heedless of the broad expanse of chest showing through the open front of his nightshirt. "The admiral almost drowned because of your selfishness, Lurlene. It wasn't easy to pull the old man out of the water. Having a broken leg didn't help!" His voice trembled as he struggled to control his anger. "I wanted to get back at you, because of the pain you caused me. My leg was set too late and healed badly. You don't know the hell—"

Lurlene tore away from Lord Bowen and rushed out of the room. Keith could not stand the accusing silence, and he covered his eyes with one hand. "That's God's truth," he said. "Please leave me alone now."

He swallowed hard as the door opened and closed. How would he face Amanda after this? She must be disgusted with him for his outburst.

After resting for a few minutes until his composure had returned, he maneuvered his legs over the edge of the bed. Pain hammered in his wound as the blood rushed to his toes, but he squeezed his lips shut against the groan that was forming in his throat. His clothes were pressed and brushed, hanging on hangers in the open armoire. The doctor had left two crutches leaning against the end of the bed.

He had to leave.

CHAPTER 16

AMANDA HAD LEFT Keith alone because she needed to sort through her thoughts. She was appalled at Lurlene's actions, and she was relieved that the truth had come out into the open. She fully understood Keith's reason for revenge; nevertheless, she didn't approve of his actions. Yet, the misery had lifted from her heart, and she wanted to speak with him and find out if his feelings—

"That is the most harebrained scheme I've ever heard!" the Dowager's voice interrupted her thoughts. "How could you, Lurlene? I'm ashamed of you."

"Enough of that, Mother," admonished Lord Bowen. "I'm sure Lurlene learned from her mistake."

Amanda sat in a chair by the fireplace in the green salon, watching Lurlene who was prostrated on the sofa, wailing. A maid waved a burnt feather above her face. The Dowagers Bowen and Waring were sitting stiffly side by side on a hard settee. The Dowager Lady Bowen looked like she was bursting with a desire to continue her harangue.

The door opened slowly, and there stood Keith, dressed haphazardly, his hair disheveled. He was leaning on two crutches. Amanda's eyes ached with unshed tears, and she wished fervently that she could put her arms around him and hold him.

He was stunned at the obvious love in her eyes. He felt his throat choke up, a sensation that had not assaulted him since childhood, and he had to blink hard to dispel the unfamiliar wetness in his eyes.

Lurlene wailed louder at the entrance of Lord Saville. She beckoned Lord Bowen with one feeble hand. "Justin, don't abandon me, don't let him come near me," she whimpered in injured tones and struggled to her feet. "I've been desolate—standing on the threshold of utter despair." With dying airs she clung to her husband.

A wave of faintness surged through Keith, and the room spun dizzily. He propped himself unsteadily against the doorjamb, seeking support from the solid wood. Everywhere he looked, curious eyes bored into him. Shrugging weakly, he said, "I would like to ask you a last favor, Lord Bowen—to send for my carriage. Then I will leave. I cannot thank you enough for your hospitality."

"Our pleasure entirely, old chap," said Lord Bowen and released Lurlene's grip on his arm. "You should not leave your sickbed so fast. Bound to make you worse. Here, come and sit down."

Keith let himself be ushered to a chair at right angles with the Dowagers' settee.

"Justin should have beaten the daylights out of you," the Dowager Lady Bowen said in a hectoring voice. "Faugh! Upsetting a perfectly good evening at Almack's with your tricks. Impudent young puppy!" She seemed to have forgotten the reason for the upset, even though she had been upbraiding Lurlene for the last half-hour. Turning to Lady Waring she said in a clearly audible voice, "Saville's a walking monument of insolence."

The marquess ignored the slur on his character and smiled at Amanda. Then he glanced at Lurlene's sulky mien.

"Lurlene, I'd like to apologize for my prank," he muttered. " 'Twas unforgivably rude."

Lurlene searched Lord Bowen's face uncertainly, and bit her trembling bottom lip. He squeezed her hand gently, and Lurlene took a deep breath.

"I suppose I treated you inconsiderately, Keith, and almost caused Admiral Riverwood's death. That was very thoughtless of me." There her lips snapped shut, mutiny filling her eyes.

A grin flashed across Keith's face. "I think we'll deal a lot better from now on." He displayed a wobbly bow and rose, aiming for the door. But he didn't get far before the nasal voice of Lady Waring halted him in his tracks. "Listen up, young man!" She waved a piece of paper in the air. "Are you the instigator of your uncle's dastardly behavior as well? Persuading him to abduct my granddaughter Pamela, I'll lay."

Lord Saville's eyes held a stunned expression as he looked to Amanda for an explanation. A small smile lurked on her lips. "Great-aunt Elfina, I don't think Lord Saville had anything to do with Sir Digby's and Pamela's elopement."

"Elopement? Dig and Lady Pamela?" Saville said feebly. He leaned heavily on the compact back of a wingchair.

"Fustian!" the Dowager Lady Bowen sputtered. "That fleshmountain loping off with my grandniece? Never! I've tried to convince all of you that Pamela will be back before nightfall. Sir Digby is too much a lover of comfort to flee headlong to the border to get leg-shackled."

"But where is she?" Lady Elfina's lips set into a grim line. "According to the note, she's been gone since dawn."

"Wherever they are now, you must see that it's too late to stop them. Has it never occurred to you that they might be in love and that they'd like to spend their lives together?" Amanda pointed out to Lady Elfina. She angled a glance at Keith, noting his dazed, ashen face. Her heart twisted with compassion. She continued, "Pamela is old enough to know her own mind, and possesses a much stronger will than she projects. This desperate action should be proof of that."

Saville collected himself, swallowing hard. "What are you talking about? I thought you and Dig—"

The Dowager snorted. "Amanda didn't know how to keep his affection. Pamela nabbed him from right under her nose."

Before Amanda had a chance to defend herself, the door opened a fraction and Pamela's bright face showed around the edge. Her cheeks were flushed with embarrassment as she stepped inside, pulling Sir Digby with her. He was mopping his forehead, evidently suffering deep worry. Upon seeing Amanda and his nephew he tried to speak, but no words came to his lips.

"Aha! He dares to put a foot in this house, that—that scoundrel, that *abductor* of young innocents," the Dowager Lady Waring exclaimed, failing pitifully to imitate her sister's stentorian voice. A very long accusing finger was directed at Digby, who blanched. His hands working the edge of his waistcoat, he said lamely, "Ahem—abductor is a very strong word."

Pamela stood squarely in front of her grandmother, her arms akimbo. "I won't tolerate you to slander my fiancé, Grandmother. Sir Digby has always behaved in a gentlemanly fashion, and if it weren't for him, I wouldn't be here right now. Had he listened to me, we would have been halfway to Scotland. And we will be—with or without your blessing."

Lady Waring looked much put-out that her little lamb was turning into a wolf right under her eyes, daring to face her grandmother with a bold ultimatum. "Well! I've never—" she said in a faint voice, placing a brittle hand to her temple.

"He blankly refused to elope—said we shouldn't go about such important business as a wedding in a havey-cavey way. *I* was the one who urged him to elope, and that only after receiving your scathing lecture last night," Pamela said in full career, hazel eyes flashing.

The Dowager cackled. "Didn't I tell you, Elfina?" She glared at Sir Digby, who looked extremely uncomfortable. "Didn't like the inconvenience, eh? Too bumpy a road, the Great Northern, I daresay."

"Now listen here!" Sir Digby began, his ire rising at last. "It was never my intention to go about this wedding in less than a proper way. Only the very best is good enough for my Pamela, and I'll see to it that she gets just that—without your high-handed interference."

"Bravo!" interjected Amanda, clapping her hands, much amused by the scene.

"And I was thoroughly shocked to hear that you disapprove of the match," Sir Digby aimed at Lady Waring in acid tones. "I know of no scandal in my family, and as for my ancestors, I don't take any blame for their actions." He puffed out his enormous chest with a deep breath. "In fact, I'm *proud* of my heritage," he said, exhaling noisily for emphasis. "And I assure you, Lady Pamela will not lack for anything."

"Consider yourself beaten, Elfina," the Dowager crowed, avidly eyeing her sister's lips working with speechless fury. She turned to Sir Digby. "Elfina's full of hot air," she explained with immense satisfaction. "Always was."

Amanda held her breath with suspense, silently praying that Lady Elfina would put the matter to rest.

The gaunt woman looked more than ever like a ruffled crow as she waved a huge black chickenskin fan in front of her face. She glowered at Lady Pamela. "Is this what you want?" she muttered. "To marry this—" she gave Sir Digby a disdainful glance, "this *pudding.*"

"Yes, Grandmother, and I'll do it with or without your consent. I am of age, after all." Lady Pamela's chin jutted with determination. "Furthermore, I won't have you calling my future husband names. It embarrasses me no end to listen to your insults. I'm surprised he even speaks with you after all the evil words you've poured over his head. And you, too," she included the Dowager.

"Very well," said Elfina. "But don't come to me and complain once you tire of his creaking corsets!"

"Grandmother!" Pamela gasped.

Amanda hid a wide smile behind her fan as the two old ladies straightened their backs and lifted their quivering noses several inches. Amanda sought Keith, curious to gauge his reaction to the heated exchange. He was leaning heavily on his crutches, his eyes half-closed. He saluted her with a mocking gesture. She flinched at his hard unsmiling stare.

"Quite a burlesque you're presenting for your guests' entertainment," he said in a frigid undertone. "I don't know how much more abuse I can take." He flung out a tired arm. "Sitting there like two black avenging angels ripping my family to shreds." Then he took a step toward the door. "Really, Amanda, I didn't think you capable of such subterfuge. You never intended to wed Dig, and you kept me in the dark all this time. After all the righteous setdowns you have given me for my conduct. You astound me," he drawled and opened the door.

Amanda flinched at his accusing words, wishing she had told him the truth in the barn outside Richmond. "It's nothing compared to your revenge on Lurlene," she hurled back. Did she ever do anything but argue with Keith? Where had that intimacy they had shared at Richmond gone?

He laughed mirthlessly. "By Jove! Little Saint Amanda. But you never mention the insults and bear-garden jaws that I have endured from your relations." He looked pointedly at the Dowager. "You don't have to suffer my presence much longer. I have no more quarrel with your family, so our paths don't have to cross further," he said in a very soft voice, for Amanda's ears alone.

She took an involuntary step toward him, desperately wanting to do something to bridge the ever-widening gap between them. "I couldn't silently stand by watching you making a fool of my father. Don't you see?"

"Justin is a capable fellow on all counts, without your *meddling*."

"How dare you!" Seething, Amanda took a step toward him.

"Frankly, I'm tired of bickering. Good-bye, Amanda." Keith hoisted his crutches over the threshold and closed the door softly behind him.

Panic seeped through Amanda. She could not let him leave for good. "Wait!" she called and rushed out the door. All that mattered now was that he would understand her true feelings.

She caught up with him in the middle of the stairs. "You must let me explain," she said. He looked pale and drawn, and she worried he would fall down the steps.

"All I want now is some peace," he grated, carefully positioning the crutches in front of him. Perspiration pearled on his forehead as he made it down the remaining steps.

"I listened to your explanation," Amanda said, touching

his arm. "Now please listen to mine." Her voice broke and she dashed a hand across her eyes.

"Very well, but help me into the carriage first. I must sit down. If I stay here, I might not get any further today."

To Amanda's surprise, the carriage was already drawn up in front of the steps. The coachman got down and assisted Keith up the step and into the coach. Amanda stepped in and pulled the door closed to shield them from probing eyes.

But before she could open her mouth, the coach jerked forward and she was pushed against Keith's strong shoulder.

"What's going on?" Keith growled angrily. "I didn't order him to drive." He glanced at the carriage as if seeing it for the first time. "Oh, my God, this is Dig's coach. Mine is almost identical, y'know."

Amanda stared at him round-eyed. "Where do you think we're heading?"

The marquess chuckled, then laughed, throwing his head back. "To the border, most likely. Dig must have given his orders in advance."

Amanda gasped. "Shouldn't we turn around?"

Keith glanced at her, a devil lurking in his eyes. "Why fight Fate? Do you have a desire to face the Dowagers further today? I sure don't."

Amanda's cheeks reddened. "You mean . . . we should *elope*?"

"I'm sure we're heading north."

A sweet tension grew between them. "Come here," Keith said hoarsely. "My leg prevents me from coming to you."

Amanda obeyed, and heaved a deep sigh of contentment as his arms closed around her. She leaned forward with great daring and put her lips to his. Desire sprung up between them, a simmering, dangerous passion. The power of his kiss intoxicated her to a point where she could scarcely breathe. He reluctantly let go of her lips and cradled her head against his chest. "Dearest termagant," he whispered. "How I suffered guilt for loving you. I was a jealous fool, resenting the possibility that you would spend the rest of your life with Digby."

Amanda smiled tremulously, her fingers curling into his hair. "We played the charade to keep Grandmama from foisting me onto some other hapless gentleman. You know how ruthless she is, and she *would* see me wed this season. Digby reluctantly obliged to the scheme since he housed mortal fears of marriage—until he met Pamela."

Saville laughed. "I suggested that he pursue you. Little did I know that I would fall into my own trap! He'll be happy with Lady Pamela." He looked into Amanda's eyes, his own filling with heart-stopping tenderness. "But I don't want to talk about old Dig—not when I have something much more important to say."

Amanda felt tears of love gather to her eyes. "What is that?" she breathed.

Steeped in ever-deepening enchantment, he whispered against her hair. "I love you, Amanda, and I want to marry you—as soon as possible. I don't want to be separate from you one more day."

Amanda swallowed hard, choking on happiness. "Yes, yes! I love you, too, Keith."

"We're birds of a feather y'know. Your plot with Dig was no less shocking than my revenge. We deserve each other." Laughing, they lost themselves in another kiss.

EPILOGUE

AFTER A LEISURELY DRIVE through the smiling countryside along the Great North Road, they spent an even more relaxed evening at a roadside inn.

"I would like to ravish you with love, Mandy, but it'll have to wait," Keith murmured against her lips as he held her before retiring to his room next to hers. "This dashed leg is taking more out of me than I thought."

"The anticipation is sweetly intoxicating, I assure you," Amanda said with a teasing smile, and blew him a kiss before closing her door.

The next morning a surprise awaited them downstairs. Upon entering the private parlor where the air was redolent with the scent of fried ham and kedgeree, they came eye-to-eye with Pamela and Sir Digby demolishing huge plates of breakfast. All four mouths fell open.

"What the deuce are you doing here?" began Sir Digby, as Lord Saville's laugh filled the room. "You stole my coach."

"Dear Uncle, I put the same question to you."

"Ahem—"

"We're in your coach," Pamela explained. "We couldn't bear the thought of having the most important moment of our lives ruined by Lurlene and the Dowagers."

"Exactly my sentiment," Lord Saville said, smiling happily. He pulled Amanda close. "Amanda has promised to marry me, so we'll be sharing the road with you."

Sir Digby rose and pounded his nephew in the back. "That is the most sensible thing you've ever done, nevvy. You're a fortunate man." He beamed at Amanda and gazed fondly at his nephew. "She'll be the making of you, Keith."

"Who would have thought an elopement would be the only peaceful way to get leg-shackled," Keith said with utter contentment.

"Looks like we're going to celebrate a double wedding, after all," said Sir Digby, "in Scotland."

Merriment shook the stout oak beams of the inn.

"Superb!" —*New York Times*

"Charming and engaging!"
—*Atlanta Journal-Constitution*

Eugenia Price's

Sweeping <u>New York Times</u> bestselling

saga of the Old South

___SAVANNAH   0-515-10486-8/$5.50
___TO SEE YOUR FACE AGAIN   0-515-10564-3/$5.50
___BEFORE THE DARKNESS FALLS   0-425-11092-3/$5.50
___STRANGER IN SAVANNAH   0-515-10344-6/$5.95

For Visa, MasterCard and American Express orders call: 1-800-631-8571

<u>Check book(s). Fill out coupon. Send to:</u>
BERKLEY PUBLISHING GROUP
390 Murray Hill Pkwy., Dept. B
East Rutherford, NJ 07073

NAME_____

ADDRESS_____

CITY_____

STATE _____ZIP_____

PLEASE ALLOW 6 WEEKS FOR DELIVERY.
PRICES ARE SUBJECT TO CHANGE
WITHOUT NOTICE.

POSTAGE AND HANDLING:
$1.00 for one book, 25¢ for each additional. Do not exceed $3.50.

BOOK TOTAL $ ____

POSTAGE & HANDLING $ ____

APPLICABLE SALES TAX $ ____
(CA, NJ, NY, PA)

TOTAL AMOUNT DUE $ ____

PAYABLE IN US FUNDS.
(No cash orders accepted.)

214B

An unforgettable and captivating romance from
nationally bestselling author

ELIZABETH KARY

FROM THIS DAY ONWARD

While The War Between the States consumed our nation in flames of bitter opposition, a single fateful moment brought Jillian Walsh and Ryder Bingham together... two strangers... two enemies... two lovers...

____*From This Day Onward*   0-515-09867-1/$4.50

Also by Elizabeth Kary:

____*Love, Honor and Betray*   0-425-08472-8/$4.50

Charlotte Beckwith and Seth Porterfield braved the War of 1812, and together forged a new life, joined by a passion as wild as the land they sought to conquer.

____*Let No Man Divide*   0-425-09472-3/$4.50

Leigh Pennington and Hayes Banister--two brave hearts drawn together amidst the turbulence of the Civil War's western front...

For Visa, MasterCard and American Express orders call: 1-800-631-8571
Check book(s). Fill out coupon. Send to:
BERKLEY PUBLISHING GROUP
390 Murray Hill Pkwy., Dept. B
East Rutherford, NJ 07073

NAME _____

ADDRESS _____

CITY _____

STATE _____ZIP _____

PLEASE ALLOW 6 WEEKS FOR DELIVERY.
PRICES ARE SUBJECT TO CHANGE
WITHOUT NOTICE.

POSTAGE AND HANDLING:
$1.00 for one book, 25¢ for each additional. Do not exceed $3.50.

BOOK TOTAL $ ____

POSTAGE & HANDLING $ ____

APPLICABLE SALES TAX $ ____
(CA, NJ, NY, PA)

TOTAL AMOUNT DUE $ ____

PAYABLE IN US FUNDS.
(No cash orders accepted.)

215

From the author of **Love, Honor and Betray** *and* **From This Day Onward** — *a magnificent new novel of desire and fear, honor and destiny . . .*

Midnight Lace

Elizabeth Kary

"A skilled storyteller!" — Roberta Gellis
"A master of the sensual historical!"
— Katherine Sutcliff

Duncan Palmer has returned to England from America for the first time since his childhood, a childhood marred when his parents were murdered. His return becomes all the more painful — he is accused of being London's West End Strangler. But help arrives for Duncan in the form of beautiful Lady Grayson. Together they will set out to find the real London murderer and his parents' killer, as well as discover a powerful love . . .

___Midnight Lace   0-515-10420-5/$4.50

For Visa, MasterCard and American Express orders call: 1-800-631-8571

FOR MAIL ORDERS: CHECK BOOK(S). FILL
OUT COUPON. SEND TO:

BERKLEY PUBLISHING GROUP
390 Murray Hill Pkwy., Dept. B
East Rutherford, NJ 07073

NAME_____

ADDRESS _____

CITY_____

STATE_____ ZIP_____

PLEASE ALLOW 6 WEEKS FOR DELIVERY.
PRICES ARE SUBJECT TO CHANGE WITHOUT NOTICE.

POSTAGE AND HANDLING:
$1.00 for one book, 25¢ for each ad-
ditional. Do not exceed $3.50.

BOOK TOTAL $ _____

POSTAGE & HANDLING $ _____

APPLICABLE SALES TAX $ _____
(CA, NJ, NY, PA)

TOTAL AMOUNT DUE $ _____

PAYABLE IN US FUNDS.
(No cash orders accepted.)

307